PRAISE FOR *THE FEVER KILL*

"It's the rare crime novel that pulsates with the nightmare intensity of *The Fever Kill*. Piccirilli pulls it off masterfully."
Charles Ardai, author/editor of
Hard Case Crime

"[A] rattlesnake-mean noir... I lost track of how many plot twists have been set out for the reader, each of them as deviously employed as a minefield. Nothing is as it seems. Sex, betrayal, violence are here—this is a noir after all— but so is a lonesomeness as poignant as a Hank Williams ballad.... *The Fever Kill* is like one sustained saxophone note, a heartwrenching wail in a Nelson Algren night. This novel is powerful, hard-hitting, fearsome stuff."
Ed Gorman, author of the Sam McCain series
and *The Day the Music Died*

"The gritty narration, graphic violence and pulp gravitas should make fans of Jim Thompson and Charlie Huston feel right at home."
Kirkus Reviews

"Piccirilli has pulled out all the stops in this vengeful drama about going home and killing everyone who done you wrong."
Bookslut

"*The Fever Kill* is great stuff! Tight, smart, with lots of good noir moves."
Jack Ketchum, author of *The Girl Next Door*

"...hardcore readers will agree *The Fever Kill* delivers.... Buy it and read an author at the top of his game who's always changing."
Bookgasm

PRAISE FOR TOM PICCIRILLI

"Tom Piccirilli doesn't just tell stories. He reaches across the page, grabs a handful of your shirt, and drags you into another world."
                    Norman Partridge, author of *Dark Harvest*
                        and *Slippin' into Darkness*

"Tom Piccirilli's fiction is visceral and unflinching, yet deeply insightful. If you miss Piccirilli you're missing one hell of a treat."
                    F. Paul Wilson, author of *The Keep*
                        and *Harbingers*

"Tom Piccirilli may write with the muscle of a 1950s paperback pulp master, but the mood and menace are totally modern. Go ahead and try to stop turning pages. You can't, even though he's got your heart on a hook and he's taken your mind places it never imagined. Piccirilli is the master of that strange, thrilling turf where horror, suspense and crime share shadowy borders. Wherever he's headed, count me in. (As long as I'm allowed to bring a gun.)"
                    Duane Swierczynski, author of *The Blonde*
                        and *The Wheelman*

"Hard, hard noir, and very well done."
                    Bill Pronzini, author of *Savages* and *Mourners*

"Tom Piccirilli is a powerful, hard-hitting, fiercely original writer of suspense. I highly recommend him."
                    David Morrell, bestselling author of *Creepers*

"[Piccirilli has] the authentic surrealist's gift of blind trust in his imagination, and that enables him to throw off striking metaphors like sparks from a speeding train."
                    The New York Times Book Review

"Relentless, mesmerizing, and just damned fine."
                    Steve Hamilton, Edgar Award-winning author
                        of *Night Work* and *A Stolen Season*

ALSO BY TOM PICCIRILLI

The Fever Kill

Tom Piccirilli

Introduction by Ken Bruen

Creeping Hemlock Press
2008 ◆ Independence, Louisiana

The Fever Kill
FIRST EDITION

First printing, Creeping Hemlock Press, January 2008

ISBN-10: 0-9769217-4-X
ISBN-13: 978-0-9769217-4-5

Cover design by R.J. Sevin and Julia Sevin
Book design by Julia Sevin
"Bleeding Teddy" spot art by R.J. Sevin

A Creeping Hemlock Press book
Editors: R.J. & Julia Sevin
Creeping Hemlock Productions, LLC
P.O. Box 2006
Albany, LA 70711

Creeping Hemlock Press wishes to thank all who contributed to the publication of *The Fever Kill*, especially Ken Bruen and Jeff Strand. Thank you for supporting recovering Gulf Coast businesses.

www.creepinghemlock.com

For Ed Gorman, Bill Pronzini,
Norm Partridge, and Ken Bruen
The nice guys of noir

The Fever Kill

Introduction

Very few writers can switch genres successfully. The few examples are outstanding purely because of their rarity and quality. Elmore Leonard moved from westerns to the best of mysteries back in the '80s and continues to break new ground. Ed Gorman is continuously shifting back and forth between genres, creating his own mixtures. Loren Estelman, Joe Lansdale . . .

But now there's a new kid on the make, switching between not only two fields but three or more. Is Tom Piccirilli mad or just a wondrous blazing talent?

Thankfully, the latter.

Tom writes like a crazed magical banshee. He evokes the sheer bliss of reading in me once again. He's written some of the most stunningly horrific, provocative supernatural novels of the last twenty years and has won numerous awards in the field because of them. His westerns and mysteries are fast, exciting, dangerous, and always heavy with the specter of darkness.

And yet, when you read his books, you're very conscious of the fact that here is an author who could—with the flip of a dime—easily write suspense, hardboiled or noir material, so closely is the tone and style allied.

And now he's done it.

Written a powerful, straightforward crime novel. *The Fever Kill.* And maybe, despite his huge talent for the other genres, this is his truest voice. Giving us an intense and astonishing piece that is as assured as if he'd been writing this sort of thing since the beginning of his career. It's as if those other dark genres were simply muscling him up for the real event.

Just maybe all that other writing was the near-perfect background for this near-perfect neo-noir voice. Taking all the ingredients that make his previous books so successful, Tom now seamlessly blends them into one hell of a gutting tale.

The Fever Kill blasts off from the first page and never lets the reader catch a breath. Those years of sharpening his skills have given a new and unique style to the crime work. Hard-honed, poetic, haunting, sharp as the fangs of a cobra, blackly humorous, and oh so damn readable.

My only regret is that he waited so long to pen this kind of novel, because this may be the dawn of a whole new era for him, and I for one can't wait to see what he comes up with after this heartfelt, brilliant book.

—Ken Bruen

Prologue

Crease had spent seven years carting his father home from barrooms and whorehouses, picking him out of the alleys and gutters and carrying him on his back through the frigid streets of Hangtree. The old ladies who woke before dawn would *tsk* loudly on their porches or smile with all the small cruelty they felt they deserved to pass back to the world. Edwards and the deputies would pace their cruisers alongside and follow mile after mile while Crease struggled beneath his father's weight. The cops would keep their dome lights on so he could see their eyes, the way they grinned. Crease didn't know who he wanted to kill more, them or his father or himself.

Sometimes Edwards would be waiting far ahead on the corner, his handsome features lit by a street lamp or the flare of a match from lighting a cigar. His golden curls drifting in the breeze, pale blue eyes burning. He'd wait until

Crease would almost reach him, and then he'd get in the cruiser and fade down a side street, leaving the butt of his cigar still glowing.

This had been going on for so long that Crease had come to expect it, and accepted it as part of a now common, familiar pain he was meant to endure.

Sometimes he would carry his father past the Groell place, old lady Virginny silhouetted by diffuse orange light in one window, the sharply-defined shape of her granddaughter Ellie in another. The two of them in different corners of the house, staring out at the darkness, waiting. For him or some other distraction or promise to come creeping up the road.

That last night—with the wintry Vermont wind slicing down out of the north hills, the blunt roar in the trees masking his grunts as he strained to get them home—Crease felt the old man begin to sob against his back.

The tears ran against Crease's neck and into his hair, steaming against his heated skin. His heart battered his chest, pulse snapping so hard in his throat that he thought the veins would burst. It would be an answer. His brow ran with feverish sweat and colors seeped at the edges of his vision.

"I didn't do it," his father mewled.

"I know that."

"The girl, Mary. What happened to her, it wasn't me."

Crease thought, If I hear this one more time I'll go insane. It may have already happened. I might have gone over the rim. How could you tell if you were on the edge or if you'd already slid over it? He might be at the bottom looking up.

"You're the only one who believes me, son."

"That doesn't matter."

"I'm sorry I brought this on you."

"None of it's your doing."

"Let me down, I gotta puke."

It was a sign of courtesy. His father had never given him a warning before. He sat the old man down on the corner propped against a mailbox and watched him throw up in the street. His father was trembling and gagging so badly that Crease began to feel as if he was doing the same. The awful noises carried on the wind and wafted through chimneys and beneath drafty doors and no one would come outside for a while. In a way, Crease was thankful.

His father slumped back, breathing thickly, an expression of panic crossing his bloated face. His chin was speckled with red foam. His eyes flitted and finally cleared. His gaze was alert but grew more and more desolate as it settled on Crease.

"I did it," his father said.

"What?"

"I think I shot her. I probably did." His father vomited again. "I never admitted it out loud before, even to myself. But I'm telling you the truth. It's time."

Crease looked and saw blood in the street.

This was it, his old man was giving his confession, right here on the curb. Crease knew he should run. He wouldn't want to hear whatever came next. Maybe he hadn't gone over the rim, maybe he was teetering. If he listened he knew he'd fall.

But even though his hips were half-turned, as if he might make a sprint for the safety of shadows, he just couldn't take that first step.

"What?" His voice sounded nothing like him, and it made him whirl to face a stranger behind him who wasn't there. "Tell me again. What did you do?"

His father didn't have much time left. Crease could see it now, how hard the man had to work to take his next breath. The blood was still coming, leaking from his nostrils and the corners of his mouth now. But he was more focused than he'd been in years. The man finally coming to some kind of an understanding, a reckoning with himself when it was too late to do any good.

"So long ago I hardly remember."

"It was seven years ago. You remember. Mom had just died. You remember it all. Tell me."

"I was waiting at the abandoned mill. Waiting to do the trade, the way the kidnappers wanted. But I opened the satchel. I'm sorry, son, I couldn't help it. Fifteen grand, we could've gotten out of this town. It wasn't much but it was enough to start over . . ." The old man beginning to falter, even now, unable to face his own actions.

Crease was seventeen. The voice—his voice now—was about a thousand years older, full of dust and ash. "Did you kidnap the little girl?"

"No, no, son."

"Who did?"

"I never found out. I searched, but I never found out." His father took a phlegm-filled breath, the blood spilling over his lips. "The only reason Edwards knew what happened is because they planned to do the same thing. I gave orders I was to be the only one there, but he was waiting, back in the woods, watching. I took out the bundles of cash and hid them in the mill. Then I sat and waited. From about noon on. Four hours, five, maybe six. It was sundown before I heard someone prowling. Probably Edwards. He must've got antsy, waiting like that, screened by the trees. Must've thought the switch had already been made and wanted to check. The door opened and I saw someone silhouetted in the sunset. I spotted the gun in his hand. We fired together. Wasn't until we started yelling that we recognized each other. By the time we straightened ourselves out, the girl was dead."

I'm being killed here, gutted, and my own father is doing it. "How?"

"She'd been there in the mill, walking around." The man's eyes filled with a furious anguish and Crease knew his father had to die now, he could never come back from this admission. "Holding a teddy bear, you see? Mary was holding her teddy bear. They'd let her go."

"Why would they do that before picking up the satchel?"

"They must've found the money I hid. They were watching. They must've been there the whole time. I don't know. But it was gone, I never even got it. Edwards ran while the girl was dying. I called it in."

All of this for fifteen grand. It didn't seem like very much, not even in Hangtree.

"You were drunk. You fell asleep."

"I don't know, maybe I did, I suppose I did."

"Which one of you shot Mary Burke?"

"I don't know, I honestly don't know." His father's words came slower, weighted by emotion. "She was shot once, and the bullet was . . . was . . ."

Crease already knew. The bullet was unrecognizable. It had gone around and around in her small body, fragmenting. He had to lean against the mailbox to keep from going over. There was blood in the street everywhere he looked.

Crease asked with his dead voice, "Did you shoot the girl on purpose?"

"No, it was an accident. It might not have been me. Maybe it was Edwards."

"Why didn't you tell anyone that?"

His father's breathing grew more ragged, the stink of his death drifting off him. Crease knew it was on him now too, this smell, and it would never go away. The old man kept pawing at Crease's leg, wanting him to get closer. Crease kneeled beside him, thinking, I should've run. Why didn't I run?

His father clawed for Crease's hand. "Nobody would've believed it. He'd just started out as deputy. Handsome as he is, golden hair, pretty boy. His parents well-to-do. Nobody'd believe my word over his."

"You were sheriff."

"Already breaking down, drinking too much. In debt because of your mother's hospital bills. My word against his. Nobody would've believed it, if I had said the truth."

"They didn't believe you anyway."

His father shuddered, moaned, and sobbed for less than a minute before he smiled with red teeth and finally died.

Two days later, at the cemetery, a priest who kept misquoting the Bible spoke for six minutes, immediately asked to be paid, complained about the cold, and strode away in his parka without shaking hands with Crease. No one else was in attendance. Crease had been naïve. Stupid, even. He thought at least a few people his father had helped before his downfall might've shown up.

Dirtwater, the deaf-mute gravedigger, could only stare at Crease in fear and heartache from the safety of tall hedges fifty yards away, wanting to do the only thing that gave his life any definition, but too scared to grab up his shovel. A welt burnished the side of his face, and his eyes shifted to Sheriff Edwards parked up on the road.

Crease's father lay there in a pine coffin wearing his only suit and tie. There was no grave dug. There would be no headstone, Crease couldn't afford one, and the county wouldn't pay. The man wasn't a fallen hero. The man was hardly a man at all.

Edwards leaned up against his cruiser gnawing on a straw, the wraparound sunglasses giving him a fashionably hip appearance. He was alone and he was smirking like there were flashbulbs going off around him. Crease looked away, then looked, and finally walked over. He thought, No matter what happens, it'll be worth it so long as I see his blood.

The voice that wasn't his own was still with him, and he figured he was going to have to get used to it. There was no fire in it even though he wanted Edwards to appreciate his hatred. But the voice remained calm and perfectly level. "You didn't have to attack Dirtwater. He never hurt anyone."

"He chose his lot."

"How so?"

"He was saying kind things about your father and poor things about me."

"He's a mute."

"He said it with his eyes."

Edwards stood there, aware of how good he looked. His golden hair in the breeze, the light hitting him just right. Cocking his smile at the perfect angle, with his muscular shoulders shrugged so high that his brown deputy's shirt was drawn tightly over his muscular chest. Crease wondered why a man so graced would willfully become so callous.

"Your father was rotten through and through, that's the truth. You know it. Let me tell you something else. He killed that girl and should've been put in prison for it. He disappeared inside a whiskey bottle because he had to choke down his guilt and shame."

"He started drinking when my mother grew ill," Crease said. The voice betrayed no emotion, no humanity. "That's why he jumped the rails."

"You're not stupid, you know the truth. He ruined your life. You're glad he's dead."

Crease wouldn't be able to hit him. He would try and fail and Edwards would unleash a torrent of swift blows that would bring Crease to his knees. He saw it all clearly in his mind long before he threw a punch, realizing it wasn't a desperate act, or even a scornful one, so much as it was a choice between doing something and doing nothing.

His fist struck bone.

Edwards cried out with a loud yawp as blood gushed from his mouth. His bottom lip was torn and a jagged piece of broken tooth had speared his cheek. The sunglasses went flying. There were those hated blue eyes. How fulfilling to see them once more. Crease struck again, shocked by the speed of his own hands, and felt Edwards' nose snap. He knew the beautiful sheriff would never be beautiful from this day on.

He took another swing and Edwards yanked loose his billy club, rammed it into Crease's stomach and chopped him over the left ear. Crease never passed out, no matter how many times he was pummeled and kicked.

They threw him in a cell and took turns beating him for three days. It wasn't so bad. They never booked him, never fingerprinted him. On the fourth day they tossed him in the back of the cruiser and drove him halfway home, then shoved him out into the street.

When he got to the house he found his backpack and his father's suitcase already packed at the curb. They'd gotten somebody who knew him pretty well to do it. His favorite clothes were inside, along with a couple of important personal belongings, including his father's badge. Maybe it had been Rebecca Fortlow, who he'd been dating on and off the past year despite her family's protests. Someone who liked him but wouldn't shed more than two tears at his leaving. Yeah, probably Reb.

Most of the furniture had been taken. He saw evidence of the neighbors' culling across the lawn: shredded clothing, flung papers, shattered dishes. What one person didn't want was left for the rest to pick through.

He walked through the house and took a shower. The shower curtain had been stolen too. There were no towels left for him to dry himself. He looked at himself in the cracked bathroom mirror and saw that they had done a damn good job of working him over. The bruises and scrapes and abrasions were terrible to see. Somehow he'd just stopped feeling their fists after a while.

When he got to the cemetery his father was still there in his coffin. Crease didn't know how to drive the backhoe, so he had to dig the grave entirely by hand. The ground was too frozen though and after fifteen minutes Crease had barely broken the soil. He siphoned gas out of the backhoe and set the ground on fire, letting it burn and smelling the sickly sweet aroma of scorched earth. Eventually the dirt softened enough that he could dig his father's grave. It took Crease almost eight hours. His hands were raw at the end of it, but there still wasn't any pain.

Crease walked to the outskirts of town, past the Groell place. It was almost midnight. Old lady Virginny must've been asleep. The window that he'd come to think of as hers was empty. But in the other, the one that was Ellie's, he saw a brief movement behind the shade. Her silhouette seemed to wag its wrist at him, waving goodbye.

He would give himself six months to get smart and strong and learn how to use a gun. Then he'd return and take a stand against the town that was all he had ever known, all he'd ever cared about, but would never again be home. Six months, and he'd settle accounts.

Instead, it took ten years.

When he returned he had an ex-wife who still loved him, an eight-year-old son who hated his guts, a row of medals he wasn't allowed to show anybody, a drug czar named Tucco on his tail, and Crease had left Tucco's mistress pregnant.

He was still trying to figure out how it had all happened and what it all meant.

Now he was strong and knew how to use a gun, but he hadn't gotten a hell of a lot smarter during his time away. He was a bent cop, like his father. The difference was, Crease was allowed to be. He didn't even have to resist the temptations of life. The narc squad paid him to join the underworld and let his darker self cut free. The worse he acted the better he did his job. What more could you ask.

In the cherry '69 Mustang that he'd rebuilt himself, ninety miles over the Massachusetts-Vermont border, fifteen outside of Hangtree, with the window open to the rain and the October night air chopping through him like when he was a kid, but sweating like hell, he decided everything would be all right, the fever would get him through.

1

Beautiful as she was, with that red, storm-blown hair dripping across her throat, fiery eyes full of anger and faint dignity, Crease didn't really notice her until he saw the blood.

She moved to the ladies' room as he hung back in the corner of the dark hall at the back of the diner, talking on the pay phone trying to get Mimi to calm down. The woman opened the bathroom door by pressing her shoulder to it and letting out a small gasp of pain as she slid inside, leaving a small swath of red against the scarred wood.

Mimi's kids shrieked in the background so loudly that he had to pull the phone away. She shouted his name repeatedly as if urging him not to forget it. "Crease! Are you still there? Crease!"

"Yeah," he told her, his gaze still on the shiny slick on the door. It had him curious. He stepped from the alcove to look out into the Truck-Mart Diner and see if there was anything going on. Cops around, a pissed off boyfriend. He saw nothing.

Mimi must've practiced being shrill. Nobody could get there on their own like this without really working at it. "Crease!"

"I'm here."

"You should be, you're the one who called me. What do you want?"

"I just wanted to know how Joan and Stevie were doing."

Mimi's breath slowly whistled out her nostrils. "You barely see either of them, you've been gone for months, and now you're phoning me to ask how they're doing? What is it with you?"

"Nothing."

"What's going on? You're getting in too deep in this undercover work, aren't you? It's messing with your head."

He'd always liked Mimi. Unlike Joan, she had a worldly crust and lots of sharp edges. She talked to him with a dark honesty that his wife had always lacked.

"Stop in and see them. Whatever you're caught up in, I think you need to come home now."

"I can't. I have to finish something first."

It took her back. She seemed to think he was talking about suicide. "But . . . but Joan and Stevie need you. They—" Even Mimi couldn't quite work up enough enthusiasm to make a real appeal. If he was on a ledge, he would've gone over by now. "What about your pension? What about your insurance?"

"Relax, I'll be back in a few days."

"You're not in the city. Where are you? When are you coming home?"

"Whenever I put an end to this thing."

"Which thing? What thing? You want to come out with it, I can hear it in your voice. But then you put up the wall. If you want to tell me, just say it. Are you drinking?"

"I'm drinking coffee, Mimi. I'll be fine. And why aren't your kids asleep yet? Go put them to bed."

"I'm going to take advice on parenting from you?"

"You should take it from somebody. Tell Joan I'm all right. And tell Stevie I love him."

"Like he'll believe me."

Crease started to hang up but the phone shook in his hand with the force of Mimi's voice, fighting him. She'd been married to a longshoreman named Lenny until five years ago when Lenny decided to throw himself in the East River one Fourth of July. Mimi was already pregnant with Lenny's fourth child by then and Crease, who was only twenty-two at the time but married for three years, a cop for two of them, had somehow allowed himself to be swept along with Joan's plans to take care of Mimi and the children.

They needed insurance. They needed coverage. He didn't know all their names but he'd legally adopted them. Or some of them. He didn't know you could do it and still wasn't sure it was entirely legal. He hadn't quite believed what was going on around him until the judge repeated Crease's name several times, just like Mimi was still doing at the moment, and asked him a few questions Crease had never answered. He'd blinked a couple times and dumbly nodded, and the next thing he knew he was suddenly the father of three or four kids. Maybe five.

Now he was twenty-seven and had a thick patch of gray growing right up in front and he couldn't remember what he'd wanted to do with his life before he'd gone undercover. Whatever it had been was now too far away.

It got confusing. He knew he was a

because they kept giving him more and more string, and forgave him for always breaking the rules. The ones they found out he was breaking. The others they didn't ask about. Even under deep cover you weren't supposed to back up the dealer during his raids on the competition, dispose of bodies, and screw the guy's mistress. Probably not, anyway.

Crease slapped the phone down onto the receiver finally cutting off Mimi's voice. They never did find Lenny's body. Crease was beginning to think that no matter how stupid Lenny had been, he'd been pretty sharp there at the end.

The woman stumbled out of the ladies' room and almost did a header into the wall. Crease's hands lashed out and caught her easily. She went slack the moment he touched her. He drew her gently into his arms, pulling her into the glow of the dim overhead light. She was completely flaccid but her intense eyes were watching him.

She had a split lip and the beginnings of a new shiner over an old one. A fresh bruise on her chin and another higher on her jaw line that was partially covered by a halfhearted sweep of flesh-colored powder, as if she'd decided there was no point in trying to cover the marks. Her hair was full of blood. He swept back the damp, waving curls and saw that an earlobe had been torn.

She said, "Well, you through looking? You can take your hands off now. Or you got something else in mind? That what this is about?" Her lips firmed so much that the cut at the corner of her mouth began to ooze again. "You want to try something?"

"Would you want me to?" he asked.

His return had already begun to affect the town, his past moving forward through time to meet him. He could very clearly see the threads of his life drawing together now, the pattern beneath beginning to emerge. There were no coincidences. From here on out, everything that happened would have resonance, like a church bell calling the lost in from the fog.

Crease said, "Hello, Reb."

She didn't recognize him, not even after she looked him up and down for a minute. He released his hold but kept a hand softly on her elbow in case she needed to be steadied. "Who are you?"

"The guy who did this, he still around? Out front maybe?"

"I asked you a question. Who are you? How do you know my name?"

He checked her eyes again to make sure they were focused, the pupils not dilated, no potential serious head trauma. She looked all right. He glanced down the hall to see if anybody out in the diner was getting inquisitive, if somebody might be heading back here to check on her. He didn't see anyone.

A bleeding redhead stumbling through the place at two in the morning. Past the waitress, the fry cook, a few truckers, a couple geezers gumming late night eggs and toast. Nobody even looked up. You'd think somebody might at least angle his neck to see if she'd snuffed it.

"We knew each other a long time ago," he said.

He realized she'd never recognize him. It was more than the gray hair and the mileage and the voice. He'd gone very far away from the kid he was over the last ten years, until even he didn't know who he was anymore.

"We did?"

"Is the guy still here?"

"I don't know," she said. "I think he drove off. What do you care?"

"Boyfriend?"

"He thinks so."

"What do you think?"

"I think he's the latest mistake in a long line of them."

He could see she regretted saying it immediately. It was flippant and coy, something a tough chick teenager might say to her sister. Her front teeth eased out over her bottom lip and she started to chew down, but the pain brought her back to herself.

She started sizing Crease up, giving him another good long once over to see what he was after, and how she might be able to play him. He'd gotten the look plenty of times on the job, from Tucco's ladies, even from Morena.

Her eye and chin were beginning to swell. He said, "Let's go put some ice on that."

He helped her walk back to the front of the diner and he put her in a booth. The waitress finally took notice and he told her to bring coffee, ice in a dishtowel, and a menu.

A pickup in the parking lot flicked its brights on, illuminating the booth in a blinding whitewash. They snapped on and off twice more before the lot went dark again.

"That your latest mistake?" he asked.

"Yeah," she said.

Crease stepped to the door of the diner and stared hard at the guy out there. The rain had stopped but that clean smell was still in the air. He breathed it in and made an effort to peel back the years on the guy to see who was under there that he might know.

Hanging out of the pickup was Jimmy Devlin, swaying high in the cab and starting to honk his horn now. He was one of the kids from the high school who used to hotrod around and throw beer cans at Crease while he was carrying his father home.

On the trip back to Vermont, Crease had thought he might have to call the minor hostilities and resentments forward, urge them from the forgotten corners. Instead, he was surprised to find all his adolescent upsets crawling free again on their own.

Despite all he'd seen on the job—the twenty-floor swan dives, the Colombian neckties, the children murdered by their own parents, the maimed innocent driven mad by rape. The homicides he'd witnessed, the bad guys he'd capped, the junkies he'd cleaned out of the river, the ocean of blood and tears, and still the petty shit from his childhood got him going.

There just had to be something wrong with him.

He still remembered how Jimmy Devlin laughed. The way he'd chirp his wheels, and kick it into fourth gear from a neutral drop so he could burn rubber down main street, the smoke drifting across Crease's face. Cars flashed through his mind until he came to Jimmy's: an orange '84 Camaro with a Cat-back exhaust system. Seated four but he'd pack his buddies in back there, the girls hanging out the windows sometimes hooting, sometimes just watching. Jimmy would occasionally lob a beer bottle high in the air and it would smash ten feet in front of Crease, exploding like a shotgun blast. The noise would rouse his father enough for him to say, in his whiskey-soaked voice, "Take cover."

Crease walked back to the table and told Reb, "Finish your meal."

"He's got a knife. He likes knives."

Crease thought of Tucco and his butterfly blade. "Everybody does."

Jimmy was going to fat. All the beer had caught up with him, and his belly hung over his belt, arms thick and tattooed and sunburned. His hair was thinning, the crow's feet really digging into the corner of his eyes. His knuckles were wide and pink. He hadn't even wiped Reb's blood off his hands.

Crease wondered how Jimmy might stack up in New York. With that swagger, the pissant rage in his eyes, the curled lip. If he walked down 112th Street throwing off sparks of attitude, some high school kid might come along and jack him with a tire iron just on general principle.

He lit a cigarette and walked past Jimmy Devlin on an angle as if he was making for the 'Stang. As their paths were about to cross, Crease turned abruptly, coming up fast, and got in close. "Hello, Jimmy."

That put a slash of a sneer across Jimmy's face. "Who the hell are you?"

You could spend your life trying to answer a question like that, asked by the people who'd spent years making you who you were. Who you'd been.

Crease said, "I'm not sure if I should believe Rebecca, so I need to ask . . . did you really slap her around?"

Jimmy liked to call his shots before he made them. He unzipped his jacket and tugged the right side back, exposing the sheathed Bowie knife attached to his belt. Crease was pretty sure that kind of presentation wouldn't hold much sway, even in Hangtree. Maybe it scared the girls.

The sneer got sharper. "Yeah, I did. You want to know why?"

"Sure."

Jimmy Devlin was a talker, he liked to tell people his whole life story. Crease had met a lot of guys like him. In fact, he thought he might be one himself. "She asked if I would help her out with her bills, which I did. Gave her four hundred bucks. Not a king's treasure, but it hurt a little.

She promised to pay me back, but I didn't care if she did. Two weeks later, she comes by my place, kicks back on my couch, gets cozy, we start getting into it. Tells me I smell and need to take a shower first. Well, all right. Except she doesn't want to come in with me. Fine. I go shave and soap up and come out to find she's taken two full bottles of Jack and stolen a hundred and eighty bucks out of my wallet. Didn't see her for another four days. Tonight she calls and says she's scared, she's stuck in a motel with a guy she doesn't remember. I go over there, get her, figure she needs some food and coffee. I stop for gas across the street and you know what she does? She runs inside and tells the kid behind the counter I need help with the pumps, something's wrong and gas is leaking. Kid comes out and she steals the plastic jug up front for the retarded kids, or maybe it was for spaying dogs. Whatever. She takes it and tries to hitch a ride with a trucker. He turns her down and she's standing there in the parking lot, holding the plastic jug. I had to talk fast to keep the kid from calling the cops, he thought I was in on it with her. I had to slug her to make her let go of the jug. There was maybe twelve dollars in it, mostly pennies. For that I'm gonna go to the pen?"

Crease stood there nodding, puffing on his cigarette. He very much wanted to beat the hell out of this guy, but the story sounded true, and the warmth he'd felt for Reb started to cool and his thoughts began to harden again. He didn't know what he owed her for saving his father's badge. He wasn't even sure it was she who'd done it.

He stared at Jimmy and remembered the crushed beer cans slapping him in the chest, the taste of it as the foam hit him in his face. The stink of the Cat-back exhaust as the engine revved and the girls in the back seat laughed. The bottles exploding. The old man lying on his back saying, Take cover.

Abruptly, Crease felt tired and the refined rage slackened at the back of his mind. He looked back to the diner to see Reb in the window, watching him. He wondered what it was that drove her to do such stupid things, one after the other, for no real profit. He figured the two of them could probably have a long talk about a lot of similar feelings.

"Okay," Crease said. "Call it a night, let it go for now."

"You act like we know each other, but I don't think we do. Who are you?"

"If I told you, you wouldn't believe me."

"Tell me anyway."

"No." The heat rose in his chest. "Now get going. Or do you have a problem with that?"

Jimmy's eyes flicked to the window and narrowed. He turned back to Crease and said, "Maybe I do."

Crease knew exactly what had happened. Reb had made another stupid bad mistake and thrown in with Jimmy again. She'd given him some kind of signal that he should take Crease out. Even if Jimmy did act out a little and punch her around some, he was knotted around her pinky. He always would be. She'd decided to deal with the devil she knew rather than take a chance that Crease might somehow be worse.

Crease said, "Hasn't she played you enough tonight? Don't be an idiot."

The diner door opened and he heard Reb's footsteps behind him.

Jimmy went for the knife. Maybe just to act tough, distract Crease, or maybe he wanted to see more blood. You couldn't always tell. You couldn't always read the truth in everybody's eyes. Some guys, like Tucco, and like the police commissioner too, said they could. They'd be there staring deep into your face, telling you they could see all of your secrets even while you told lie after lie until your mouth was dry.

So Jimmy was going for his knife. Still.

Reb's footsteps stopped on the walk behind him, and he sensed she was deciding which way to go, how to make it out of here. He could feel her fear as naturally as he might feel his own, even though he wasn't afraid of anything. He heard her hair wafting in the wind, the blood, knotted clump of curls tapping against the side of her face.

There was Jimmy, still reaching.

Maybe Crease had just become jaded after seeing Tucco snatch out his butterfly blade and strike like a snake with it, going for the eyes and the neck and the temple. One jab, that's all he ever needed. Twisting the blade a little to make sure the damage was done, then yanking it back out, snapping the knife shut and replacing it in his pocket so quickly he never got a drop of blood on himself.

Finally, Jimmy was almost finished pulling the Bowie, coming up with it. More of a defensive posture than a killing stance. He really didn't want to hurt anybody. It was all show. Another stupid move. You don't pull a deadly weapon without meaning to use it.

Crease stepped forward and chopped the side of his hand down hard on Jimmy's wrist. The knife dropped and Crease caught it by the handle before it had fallen three inches. He decided to keep it.

His free hand flashed out and yanked the sheath off Jimmy's belt and put it on his own. He stuck the Bowie in its sheath while Jimmy stared at him in terror.

"Go away now," Crease said.

But Jimmy—like Reb, like Crease's father, maybe like Crease himself—could only compound the problem by making yet another bad move. The stupidity latched on and drove you further and further into hell. You hit the gas instead of the brake. You reloaded instead of putting your hands up.

Jimmy Devlin gathered up his remaining anger and lifted one of those large fists and swung it up from his knees. The fist rose and rose, the arm straightening as Jimmy hauled off. His body twisted and he let loose with a grunting war cry like he expected to kill Crease or be murdered in the next ten seconds. He actually closed his eyes and turned his face, afraid to see where the fist might go.

Crease thought, I'd have to wait here all night long before that punch came anywhere near me.

He stepped in and still had to wait before Jimmy's wrist came up far enough that Crease could snap his forearm against it. He tapped Jimmy twice in the solar plexus, twice more on the chin, and watched the guy's eyes roll up into his head.

An icy wind blew dead leaves across Crease's knees, the scent of the past coming on even stronger now. He turned away before Jimmy hit the ground.

On the walk, Reb stood unsure of what to do, which way to run. The cool acceptance in her expression had almost given over to an animal panic.

She struggled with it for a second before coming to the realization that Crease wasn't about to beat on her, wasn't even going to make her explain herself.

He opened the passenger door of the 'Stang and said, "I'll give you a lift home. Or do you want to stay here?"

She started to relax a little, and the adrenaline buzz she'd been on dissipated. The exhaustion flooded into her face and he had to sling himself forward as she pitched into his arms again.

He got her into the 'Stang and drove north toward Hangtree. Reb showed him her teeth, said, "Crease, god-damn you, it's been a while," and passed out against the dashboard.

2

He drove easily through the back roads on the outskirts of town, the intimacy returning to him with the slippage of memories. They came to him sharply and ground inside him like broken glass, a particularly jagged recollection making him frown or tighten his fists on the steering wheel.

Reb didn't carry a purse, but he figured she still lived in the same house where she'd grown up. Where he used to climb the trellis to her window and ease into darkness, and she'd urge him on with faint murmurs and throaty laughter. With only a sliver of silver moonlight slicing through a broken pane to show him the way. He'd stumbled on the icy shingles once and busted the corner of the window with his knee. From then on, a cracked crescent shadow always hung across his back as he slid into bed with her. Her father would get up in the middle of the night and play videotaped reruns of old baseball games. Reb's fingers would be working through the sweaty folds of Crease's chest hair, and he'd hear the man cursing and thumping the arm of his recliner like he still had a bet on the game.

There was hardly any growth to Hangtree. He spotted an extra gas station, another street light, and about five acres of new housing development sidling toward the highway. Everything else was pretty much how he remembered it.

He parked in front of Reb's house, a little stunned to see the place in such sad shape. The rain gutters had collapsed and lay hanging against the sides of the house, swaying slightly in the wind. The porch had severe water damage, stairs and floorboards chipped and buckling. The screen door had busted off its hinges and stood propped under the outside light. Straw spun from disintegrating birds' nests jammed in the high corners of the veranda. The yard was overgrown, heavily choked with weeds and leaves. A maple had fallen and crushed a ten-foot portion of the back fence. It looked like it had happened at least a couple of years ago. He felt a strange tug of sorrow.

So Reb's parents were dead. Her old man, for all his faults, was always on the ball when it came to home repair and taking care of the place.

Crease looked over at her snoring thickly through her swollen nose. He knew she lived here alone with the ghosts of her mother and father cloying the rooms, wandering the halls, seated at the kitchen table.

He glanced up and saw the broken window. The crescent crack had spiderwebbed out to consume the whole pane.

Sometimes you found the symbols of your life, and sometimes they found you.

He got her out of the 'Stang and half-carried her to the front door while she murmured plaintive appeals. She muttered questions and answered them herself, crying out, "No way, hell no." He didn't know her body anymore and had trouble relating the plump, curvy teenager with this skinny, hard, lovely woman. Their combined weight bowed the rotted porch. The stink of fetid water rose from beneath the house.

The front door was open and the minute she got inside she relaxed again and went totally limp. She was easier to handle that way. He lifted her as she slumped into the crook of his arm, and he went through the place turning on light switches, her feet brushing dust from the furniture. On the walls, antique portraits with austere expressions kept an eye on him. The dead were always watching.

He got her on the couch, searched the bathroom and kitchen and found a dishtowel, ice, coffee, aspirin, bandaging tape, and hydrogen peroxide. Reb's breath whistled through her nose. He checked it and found it wasn't broken. He peered into her mouth to make sure her jaw wasn't dislocated and no teeth were cracked. She'd be all right.

The sink was stacked with dirty dishes. She didn't have a microwave or a coffee pot so he had to wash out a mug and pour the stale grounds in and fill it with hot water. He got the aspirin down her throat and made her take a few sips of coffee. He pressed the dishtowel full of ice onto her face, cleaned the torn earlobe, and got some tape on it. She could use a stitch but he figured she'd never go to a doctor. He did the best he could.

He sat beside her and looked at her father's chair. It was about three feet from the television, the arms pounded all out of shape. He wouldn't even have to ask her what happened. He knew the man had died right there, in front of the TV, screaming at the screen.

Her mother, a petite, weak-willed woman with sagging shoulders, would've died shortly after him. She probably spent his funeral feeling overwhelming relief and hope, thinking there was still time to do something with her life. Crease could just imagine her staring in the mirror, trying to force herself to accept the idea that she was still pretty enough to start again. Young enough. Strong enough. *Almost.* The world would've loomed large and mysterious for her after so many years in the house, acting out her role in carefully produced movements. The dishes, the dusting, the baking of pies, her existence defined by the concise repetition of endless minutiae. The thrill of freedom would begin to vanish, slowly at first and then more rapidly, as her despair mounted. *How do you start? What do you do?*

No wonder Rebecca cut loose like a wildcat. Her parents were gone but she was living in the vault full of their memories. She'd have nowhere else to go but she'd still never want to go home. She'd stay out all night long with anybody, just so long as she could stay away from the place. The sex and stealing and late-night slap-arounds would just make life a bit more fun and bearable.

He noticed she was awake and watching him. She stirred beside him on the couch and groaned.

"Are you going to jump me?" she asked.

"Would you want me to?"

"You said that before."

"It's the same answer to the same question."

She thought about it. "I don't know. I don't think so. Not tonight anyway."

"Just as well."

A woman who'd spent years throwing only one thing around didn't like to have it thrown back. A red shadow crossed her face. "What do you mean by that?"

"It means I don't feel like jumping you, Reb. Not tonight anyway."

"Why not?"

"It's been a long day."

She shook her head at him like he was crazy.

They all judged you and found you wanting. The pervs and the misfits, the dealers and the addicts. A guy who'd just raped a grandmother would still give you the stink-eye.

Now here Crease was, with a beaten girl living in a rotted home, and she was staring at him like he was nuts. Where did it come from? This complex they all had, thinking they were better than the next person even when they were down in the sewer. Sometimes it made him laugh. Sometimes it didn't.

He lit a cigarette and sat there smoking in silence. It was weird, but he only smoked in front of other people, never when he was alone. What the hell did that say about him? He shifted so the sheathed knife wouldn't dig into his thigh.

She stared into his face and said, "Why are you back? Why in God's name would anybody come back?"

"I've got unfinished business."

"It's been, what, ten years?"

"Yeah."

"Any business you can let go for ten years *is* finished."

It wasn't true, not quite anyway, but he didn't blame her for thinking so. He'd performed CPR on dying men who lived long enough to confess to sins from forty, fifty years ago. Talking about crimes that were so old they weren't even on the books anymore. Begging forgiveness from their long-dead wives, friends who wouldn't even remember their names. Some of it never got finished.

"You could've killed him," she said. "Jimmy. The way you took his blade away from him. You handled him like he was nothing."

He thought she'd ask why he hadn't. Why he hadn't killed a guy he had nothing against anymore except the vestiges of an adolescent venom, as if it was the normal thing to do. You meet a guy in a parking lot and you get a little steamed so you take him out of the game. The modern world was an impatient place. It wanted you to run to extremes.

But she didn't ask. She stretched her legs out over his lap and he began rubbing her calves, the way he used to do with Joan back when they were first married. She'd coo and moan with pleasure and eventually sit up and slide into his lap and they'd make love. He'd hold her tight like he was sinking into a well while she panted in his ear.

"You got a wife?" Reb asked.

"Divorced."

She nodded, as if it were the only answer she ever heard. "Kids?"

"Yeah."

"How many?"

"I don't know," he told her. "Six or seven, I think."

She smirked at him. "You a strutting tomcat now? How the hell can you not know how many kids you have?"

It was another good question. He said, "I legally adopted my sister-in-law's kids. My wife asked me to. It seemed like the right thing to do. I was trying to be everything my father wasn't. I have an eight-year-old son named Stevie. He's very smart and extremely mature. He hates me."

"Why's that?"

"I walked out on them, more or less, a few years back."

"Why?"

"It was part of the job."

"Which job?"

No reason to tell her anything but the truth. "I'm a cop."

It got her nodding again. "Like your father," she said.

"Yes, like my father."

Thinking that, except for the man's one big mistake, he'd always been pretty clean. The weight of the world had broken him down a piece at a time. Crease's mother's death had been the final crush.

Crease thought, Me, I get to party and deal drugs and double-tap bastards to the back of the head, and I get paid for it from both sides. I have medals that I can never wear, not that I'd want to.

"Why did a cop have to walk out on his family?" she asked.

"I was undercover. I had to build a whole new life."

"I didn't think they gave cops with families that kind of job."

"They don't," Crease told her. "I ran into a dealer named Tucco one night in a bar. I made up a name on the spot. We got to be friends. Pretty soon he was inviting me back to his penthouse to meet his posse. Most of them were low-level traffickers, but a couple were the real thing. Guys moving two hundred keys a year. Big scores. Without even trying I was hanging out in his inner circle. The department had been trying to place a man undercover in there for a couple years but Tucco always sniffed them out."

"So why didn't he sniff you out?"

"I don't know. Maybe because I was never much interested in busting him. I liked him, we had some good times."

"How old was your son then?"

The question took him back. He stopped rubbing her legs and lit another cigarette. "Almost six."

"You didn't give them up for the job. You liked your new life. The drugs and money and women, right?"

There was no way to explain it to her. She had small-town reasoning. She thought it was all about cash and getting laid because that's all there was to reach for in a place like Hangtree. She'd never understand what real action was. How your nerve endings were always on fire. How, no matter who you were with, you had to look over your shoulder, had to always be ready for the double-cross, the knife in the neck. Had to stay sharp. Crease never did any drugs and Tucco liked that about him, that he could be just as crazy without getting high as the other guys were when they got wasted. It was all part of being out on the rim. He couldn't trust his captain or the commissioner any more than he could trust Tucco. Maybe less.

Reb let out a throaty laugh full of base assumptions. "You traded in your old lady and eight or nine kids for the chance to roll around in the big life. To take a pop in the vein, drive the best cars, wear diamond pinky rings. Strippers and whores all the time." She stared through him, not seeing him at all. Seeing somebody else completely. Is that what she thought the long green got you? Pinky rings? "You like the dirty life."

"Mostly," he admitted. "They're better off without me anyway. Joan needs a different kind of man, someone who can give her a stable life. Someone who comes home at a decent hour, who puts in his time around the house. Makes sure she's not alone too often. I was never very responsible. She's a very good mother, to Stevie and to me too, when you get down to it. She deserves somebody better."

"You're getting maudlin."

"Yeah. Being back in Hangtree is doing it to me."

She groaned as she struggled to sit up. He helped her get to her feet. She took more aspirin and downed the rest of the coffee. "You got any bags? Clothes?"

"No, nothing."

"You didn't plan on coming back here, did you?"

"It just sort of happened."

She gave him the eye, led him upstairs and said, "You can take my parents' room, right here. Has its own bathroom and shower. Not much of my father's will fit you, but anything that does you can have. I'm down the hall."

"I remember," he said.

He dreamed of Mary Burke, the girl his father had killed.

She was four or five years younger than him, but he vaguely remembered her from grammar school recess, when all the grades came out to play together. Burnished copper hair and large, almond eyes. A girl who usually sat alone watching the others without jealousy or interest, who preferred her own company. She usually carried a doll or a teddy bear. He was ten when he heard the news his old man had accidentally iced her.

In his dreams she was always bleeding and lying in his arms and the playground was covered with crows. Sometimes he was yelling and sometimes he was attempting to soothe her while she sobbed. When he dreamed he'd tussle and kick and lash out. He'd wake up with his own voice in his ears and Joan would be holding her arm, her breast, asking him if he was all right. That's what kind of woman she was. Joan would stare at him and he'd know he'd had another of the dreams, but she would never tell him what he'd said, if he'd said anything at all. It wasn't until Morena that he found out that he'd cry out, *You're my sister, Mary.* Morena took it literally, thinking his old man had screwed around on the side and Mary was Crease's half-sister.

Crease figured it meant that in his heart he knew his father had tied him to the little girl, making her a part of his life forever. The same way that Crease had made Morena a part of his life. Morena, the baby, even Tucco and his gunman Cruez. You couldn't make it through the world without a family. If you didn't have a family, you made one out of whoever was around, plucking them from out of the air.

Mary Burke dying over fifteen grand. His father destroyed. Crease's mother gone, his adolescence dragged into hell, all for such an insignificant sum. Tucco used to carry twice that in his money clip, in hundreds, so he could tip the strippers a C-note at a time.

He awoke in the deep night and found Reb in bed with him, nude, laying back against the headboard, staring at him with the moonlight skipping playfully across her face. The wind had risen even more and the maples out front were swinging their branches in a savage dance.

"You want the money, don't you? That's why you're back."

"What money?"

"The money your father stole and hid."

"If he'd taken the money, he wouldn't have died a drunk in the gutter."

"There must've been a reason. Everyone knows he shot that girl and took the ransom money."

"They do, eh?"

"Yes, and so do you."

"He said he hid it and it was stolen from him."

"So you do want it."

"I want to know who wound up with it. I want to know why fifteen grand was enough to cost a girl her life."

"Hell, that's more than enough reason to lead to murder anywhere, much less in Hangtree."

She was right. He'd seen some of the Colombians take out a guy's eye for skimming a grand or two off the top. Crease had to remind himself that nobody really needed a reason to start a massacre. People were always reaching for some kind of answer.

"You're going to kill him, aren't you?" she asked.

"Who?"

"Sheriff Edwards."

Crease thought about it for a minute. "Maybe."

"Why do you say it like *that*?"

"Like what?"

"Like you don't really care one way or another."

"I don't know."

"You could've killed Jimmy pretty easily. He's considered tough around here."

"He's not."

"You kept his knife. I like that. Taking it away from him like a kid who's been bad and doesn't deserve his toy."

"I'm going to need a knife soon," Crease said.

"Why?"

It would come down to him and Tucco playing around with blades. As much as he tried, he just couldn't see himself shooting Tucco. There'd be a lot of talk and a lot of build-up, even some laughter along the way, but in the end Tucco would lash forward like lightning and Crease would have to be ready for it.

3

He went to visit his father's grave.

The 'Stang wanted to cut loose beneath him, and he found it difficult to keep it under control. Driving through Manhattan was hellish with a light on every corner. Back here, you had hundreds of miles of back road without even a stop sign. The 'Stang was tuned fine, he'd burn past any of the local cruisers. It might be fun, running Edwards and the others around the county for a few hours, just for the hell of it. Do some of the idiot things he hadn't been able to do as a kid.

He took it slow across town and passed by the police station, keeping an eye out. He didn't see anyone he recognized, and at the next light he pulled a hard left and tromped the gas pedal.

The area grew lush with wild maple and the seething, fiery colors of the dying leaves. The tourist traffic would be heavy for another couple of weeks. Families on road trips through New England, kids hunting through the pumpkin patches. The last of the maple syrup for the season would be going out in buckets before it got too cold.

The high arching gate-work narrowed his attention as Crease slowed, turned off the road, and drove past the spear-point fencing and brick pillars into the cemetery.

He parked and threaded his way to his father's grave, each step somehow calming him instead of bringing the fever forward. He felt like he was doing something wrong, that he might not care enough to actually accomplish what he'd set out to do. His resolve seemed to be waning. Strange that should happen here, where he'd buried his own father and been run out of town.

The old man's grave had sunken in about a foot. Crease hadn't packed enough of the frozen earth back into the hole that night. The yellow grass on it grew in scruffy patches. There was no tombstone, but Dirtwater, or someone, had put a few large rounded rocks where the headstone should be. The spring rains had dragged mud up against them to form a kind of knobby crest.

Dirtwater was busy fifty yards off trimming some brush, his back to Crease. A boy of about eight years old held onto a rake with a wooden handle taller than he was, smoothly drawing leaves and sticks into a pile.

Crease leaned up against a tree, lit a cigarette, and wondered what it was that had driven him all this way, non-stop, from New York. Some kind of mild need for revenge that, at the moment, he didn't quite feel anymore. His father's apathy was still affecting him through all the years, even from his own death. Crease had fallen into the same rut he'd been in when carrying the man on his back through the streets, when nothing could anger or harm him.

"Hey!"

Crease turned and saw the boy was rushing toward him. He had a nice fluid way of moving, trained not to step on the graves. He nimbly maneuvered through the aisles and skimmed past the clutches of angels and virgin mothers with outstretched arms.

"Who are you?" the kid asked. "If you don't mind me asking."

"I don't. I'm Crease. How about yourself?"

"I'm Hale. You're not supposed to smoke here."

"Why?" Crease said, genuinely curious.

"We had a dry summer and the fall's no better. There's been some bad brush fires. There's a ban on smoking in wooded areas."

Crease wouldn't exactly call the graveyard a wooded area, but he decided not to argue with the boy. He put his cigarette out on the heel of his shoe and, not wanting to throw the butt on the ground, replaced it in his pack.

"Are you Dirtwater's son?"

"Yep."

"You look just like him."

The boy smiled. "He tells me I look like Mom. He says that's a good thing, since he's ugly. But I know he's not. He's not really handsome, even Mom knows that, but he's not ugly, not too ugly anyway, so I'll take what you said to me as a compliment."

The kid liked to talk and showed a real maturity, just like Stevie. "Good, because that's how I meant it, Hale."

"So thank you."

"You're welcome."

Dirtwater didn't know how to do sign language, but through expression and gestures, he could hold a pretty damn good conversation. It was a nice balance that he should have a boy who enjoyed talking so much, and was so good at it.

"I'd like to talk to him," Crease said.

"Do you know my Dad?"

"I did a long time ago."

He was worried that Dirtwater wouldn't remember him. Crease couldn't even show him any identification, since all of it was in his cover name. All he could do was flash his father's badge at him, which wouldn't mean anything. Maybe point at the old man's grave.

But when he looked over again Dirtwater was already staring at him. Those dark expressive eyes showing recognition. Dirtwater smiled and opened his arms, waving both hands. Despite himself, Crease let out a laugh.

They shook hands and Crease was surprised at Dirtwater's strength. He'd run up against guys a lot tougher but none of them contained the same kind of immense inner power that Dirtwater exuded. Crease imagined it must have been very hard for him to have taken that punch from Edwards ten years ago and not broken the deputy's neck.

Crease didn't know what to say or how to say it. Dirtwater could read lips perfectly, but Crease couldn't find any words. All this way and now here he was face to face with another person from his past, but anything he might ask or tell him seemed moot. There was too much significance in the moment and also not enough.

He cocked his head and Dirtwater grinned and nodded, patted him on the shoulder and gave him a brief hug. Dirtwater gestured, his hands fluttering, his eyes and features shifting expression. Crease looked back over his shoulder at his father's sunken plot.

Hale told him, "He says he knew you'd show up again one day. He's been waiting for you."

"He knew more than me then."

Dirtwater's lips were moving, but since he'd never heard speech and couldn't actually talk, Crease didn't grasp how these could be actual sentences. But Hale watched him carefully and obviously understood. "He says he can see your sadness. You waited too long."

"I originally planned on six months. Time got away from me."

"He says you're not who you're supposed to be."

That straightened Crease's back. Hard enough hearing such things inside your own head without some deaf mute saying them to you, by way of his chatty son. Crease wanted another cigarette. "That's probably true of any of us."

"More so for you, he says."

Crease stared into Dirtwater's eyes. You could witness a lot in Dirtwater's face. His silence allowed for a great deal of sudden contemplation, and the hush of the cemetery only added to it. He tried to read the man's face but only saw something of himself there, a cloudy reflection. Maybe Dirtwater was doing it on purpose or maybe it was just his natural skill at communicating without a voice.

Crease let out a little grin, the one that Tucco's people knew to beware of, and Dirtwater's face closed up like a fist.

Hale said, "He's not saying anything."

"Good. I want to see where Mary Burke is buried."

Dirtwater and the boy wafted between headstones like ghosts. Crease followed, tripping over roots and chuckholes, catching his jacket on fat little angels' wings.

Hale was in the lead and Crease wondered why the kid should know where Mary's grave should be. Crease got that feeling again that his past was rushing forward to encompass and color and affect the present. That every move he made was the completion of some small action started ten years ago.

"Here," Hale said.

The stone was plain. It simply said: *Mary Burke, Beloved Daughter, Taken From Us Too Soon.*

"She mean something to you?" the kid asked.

"I don't know."

"How could you not know if a dead girl means something to you?"

Dirtwater drew the boy back by his arm and pressed a finger over the kid's lips. The three of them stood there like that for a while, Crease enjoying the breeze blowing against the back of his neck.

He knew he would never know who kidnapped her. He'd never be sure of where the money went or even if his father had truly shot the girl. Some mysteries you're not meant to answer. Some of them are supposed to continue on and on, tainting your life.

There would never be an end to this for him, and it didn't really matter, he was just killing time. But he decided he would visit with her family, ask questions, nose around a decade and a half too late.

It wasn't to make amends for the old man. He could never do that and wouldn't bother trying. But he'd come back here for some reason and he figured this might be a part of it, and anyway, he had a day or two until Tucco showed up.

Hale brushed against Crease's arm. "He wants to know if your father picked her up . . . no, took her . . . like everybody thought."

Crease looked over at Dirtwater. "No, but he planned to grab the money, only somebody beat him to it. Edwards was there, in the woods, but my father didn't think he got his hands on it either. It vanished from the mill that night. Either the real kidnappers got it or somebody else did."

Dirtwater furrowed his brow, moved his hands and fingers, made sharp gestures in the air. "He says you should forgive your dad."

"I have, a long time ago."

"If you want, I can put some flowers on her grave. On his too, if you want."

"That would be nice, Hale." Crease got out his wallet and held out a twenty, but the boy didn't take it.

"Don't cost anything to pick flowers."

Crease stood there for a while longer, and then he turned and watched the kid staring at his father with such obvious love and he thought of himself at that age staring up at his own father. Then he thought of Stevie and how much his son already despised him, and he knew the hate would only gain greater purchase and continue to build within him through the years. Even if Joan found another man—a good man this time—and got remarried, the guy would never be able to reach beyond Stevie's rage. Crease would have to do something to save his son, but he didn't know what it might be.

Crease was driving slowly through town again, riding past the station with his foot itching to floor the pedal, when a cruiser wheeled out of a parking slot in front, screeched in reverse over the double yellow line, and gunned up beside the 'Stang.

"You," the cop said through his open driver's window. "You've been roaming around town all day today, haven't you." It wasn't really a question.

"Yes sir, I have," Crease said. He let it roll easily off his tongue, the way he did when he was in uniform.

"Alone. Most folks who come through here are with their families. Who are you?"

Crease gave him the other name. Until he said it he wasn't even sure that he remembered it, although he'd been using it for more than two years. The cop would already have his tags and the name would match up to them.

"Who are you?" Crease asked.

"I'm Sheriff Edwards."

Crease kept his face blank but it startled the hell out of him. He couldn't believe it. Edwards appeared to have aged twenty years over the last ten. The broken nose had never been set right, and it had been broken a couple more times since Crease had tagged him. He'd gone to seed, had gone so soft that Crease couldn't do much besides study him, noting all the disagreeable details. The wet, alcoholic puffiness in his face distended his features like a balloon stretched too thin. He looked more than a little like Crease's father at the end.

God damn.

"So let me ask you, son," Edwards said. "What are you doing in my county?"

"Visiting a friend."

"And just who might that be?"

You had to give it to him, the man could smell intent, his senses as sharp as an animal's. "Rebecca Fortlow."

"I know most of Reb's friends. She doesn't have many of them."

"Regardless, I am one."

"Then you're definitely up to no good. That girl is nothing but a mess of trouble."

Crease kept silent.

"Why don't you get on out of here now, son? Reb's had enough problems without all you boys chasing her farther off the narrow path."

Crease kept silent.

"You hear me, son?"

"Yes, sir," Crease said.

Edwards sat back in his seat and sucked his teeth, eyeing Crease closely. This was the moment when it could go either way. Edwards seemed about to make a move and then decided against it. He was going to play it smart and wait and see just what kind of trouble Crease brought to town.

"Now you drive careful in this county."

"I will, sir."

"Oh, I know you will."

Crease drove slowly away and watched Edwards in the rearview wheeling across the double yellow again and backing into his spot. Crease wondered what the man would've done if he'd told him his true name.

4

When he got back to Reb's house he saw that she'd spruced the place up. She'd spent some time on herself, used better-applied makeup to cover the worst of the bruises. The swelling was almost completely gone. He knew she was already trying to tempt and bait him for whatever she might be able to get, and he liked the fact that their relationship had such clearly marked parameters. You were safe so long as you knew where you stood.

She moved to him with an easy grace today, sweeping along like she was dancing. It was the way she used to move, how he remembered her coming into his arms when they were teenagers and spent most of their time talking in whispers against each other's necks.

"What did you do today?" she asked.

She didn't say it the way Joan used to say it, like he might actually be able to tell his wife what he'd done on the job. She'd be standing there in the kitchen stirring batter in a bowl, expecting him to discuss a strangled baby in a bassinet or some crack whore who'd been selling her children out of the back room. Joan just smiling so beautifully and vapidly at him, the bleached white apron trailing across the bottom of her sun dress. The batter whipping around and around and around. It would make Crease so nauseous he'd have to back away into the bathroom.

Reb asked with a real understanding, aware that he was on the hunt, that he had to chase something down. He told her about the cemetery, Dirtwater and the boy, running into the sheriff.

"Why didn't you kill him?" she asked. "That's what you wanted, right?"

He looked at her. "You're having fun, trying to get into my head, aren't you? I can tell you're enjoying yourself."

"You're a break from the usual, I'll say that much."

"I never said I wanted to kill him."

"You never said you didn't either. If you don't want him dead, what's the point of coming back?"

"I don't know."

"You are a very confused soul."

His course seemed very clear, he just didn't know to what purpose, what he might get out of it in the end. "I want to know who kidnapped Mary Burke and what happened to the money."

"And if your father really shot her."

"He said he did. I believe him."

"My god, killing a child."

"Yeah."

The man was already on the downturn, but that night finished him. Maybe because of shooting Mary Burke, maybe just because he'd missed his chance at the fifteen grand score. Crease had tried to give the memory of his father the benefit of the doubt, but the more he thought about it, the longer he was a cop, the less he figured icing the kid had anything to do with it. His father had wanted that fucking money.

He sat on the couch and Reb drew up alongside him, slinky and soft enough to get his head turning to other thoughts. Like he didn't have enough on his mind, all he needed was another woman, maybe another kid.

"Did you rob him?" she asked.

"Now who we talking about?"

"The dealer you were pals with. Did you steal any of his cash or his drugs?"

"No," Crease said.

That stopped her. She drew her chin back, giving him a quick once-over like she had to reassess. Then she grinned. "I don't believe you. I bet he's after you right now because you stole a briefcase that belonged to him. Stuffed with cash. How much? A hundred grand? Two hundred?"

"He used to offer me that much to go kill competitors, guys using the harbor a little too freely, but I always turned him down."

It was the truth, but not all of it. Crease used to walk side by side with Tucco and Cruez into apartments where they knew the competition had closets full of uncut coke, maybe a thousand vials of crack. In the bathroom a do-it-yourself meth lab. He never took money for it, but he did it anyway. One day he helped Tucco take down a five-man Colombian crew that was edging into his turf. They got the name of a major connection. Crease wouldn't take any cash for it, but he did spend the night with three of Tucco's ladies, thinking of Morena the whole time. It was a bad night. Three days later, the commissioner decorated him in a private ceremony, shook his hand, patted his back, gazed on him fondly. Cameramen took photos that could never be printed. Crease thought that if his father was only half as confused as he was himself, it was no wonder the old man had gone over the big edge.

"Then why do you think he'll be coming after you? If you didn't take anything from him?"

"You wouldn't understand."

"Explain it to me."

Crease wouldn't be able to, but he gave it a shot. "It's part of the whole situation. He can't let me walk out."

"Why not?"

"It's not in his nature."

"Sounds like you boys don't play a much different game than folks around here. Than guys like Jimmy. Nobody likes to lose. It's hard enough looking in the mirror."

It was true. The game was faster and nastier but essentially the same.

"You want to go to bed?" she asked. She started to unbutton his shirt, working her fingers in his chest hair, the way she used to do, and then over his flat, muscular belly. His stomach rumbled and she drew her hands back as if she'd been stung.

He said, "How about a steak?"

She had nothing in the fridge so Crease went into town again, to buy some food. The supermarket had a couple of nice sirloins.

He had just put the last bag in the trunk of the 'Stang when he glanced up the street and the heat began to crawl across the back of his neck.

A bulky guy a little too dark for Hangtree was walking towards him with his hands in his coat pockets. It threw off his swaggering walk a little. His eyes were focused down and to the left, so that Crease was in his peripheral vision the entire time. The guy only looked up when he was about ten feet away. He smiled in what was supposed to be a disarming fashion, but it gave him a kind of animal leer.

This one was the first wave of muscle. This one wasn't supposed to survive. Tucco was sending him in just to get an idea of what Crease was capable of. To see if he'd relaxed any. Tucco and Cruez would be waiting at the other end of town, near the highway, where they could bolt if they had to make a run.

Crease reached under the dash to the magnetic drop box where he kept his .38 hidden. He plucked it free just as the guy came up very close, crossing the line of personal space. Muscle liked to get in close. They felt comfortable there, thinking they were so imposing that everybody else would just freeze in fear.

"Excuse me, buddy, but you—"

There was some foot traffic around so Crease had to be fast. He brought the butt of his gun up against the guy's forehead twice. It staggered the thug enough to make him completely pliant but didn't knock him out. His hand came free from his coat and a butterfly knife rolled down the length of his fingers and clattered on the street.

Tucco and the butterfly knives, always with the knives.

They looked cool but took too long to get out, all that whirling and snapping, and they were messy as hell to put away after being used. Crease picked the blade up quickly, pulled the guy by the elbow around to the passenger side of the 'Stang and stuffed him inside.

The thug had one wide hand clasped over his head wound and blood was seeping out from beneath it.

Crease said, "Don't bleed on the seat."

Nobody on the street had seen anything. Crease got in the 'Stang and drove in the opposite direction of Reb's, back up to the highway. Tucco and Cruez would be around, pulled off on the side, maybe drinking tequila and listening to something with a good salsa beat. They'd look up and see Crease drive by and start laughing, give him a chase before dragging ass back to whichever motel they were holed up in. Morena would be in the back seat taking it all in, making plans of her own.

Crease hit the highway and didn't even bother to check the rearview. He opened it up and within half a minute hit triple digits.

This was a no man's land of road. Edwards and the county cops wouldn't patrol it because it was supposed to be covered by the state troopers. It wasn't worth their time trying to take bribes on the border of their jurisdiction. The troopers didn't care much about a stretch with no other major town around and hardly anyone coming through anyway. Even tourist season didn't bring in much traffic. Nobody wanted to circuit boonie turf.

Crease floored it nearly all the way back to the diner where he'd first seen Reb again, until the interstate connection came up and the trucker traffic got thick again.

The thug still had one hand pressed tightly over the wound. Blood dribbled down his face and collected in his collar. Crease found a rag under his seat and gave it to him. "Here, staunch the flow with this. What's your name?"

"You gonna kill me?"

"You want me to?"

"No."

Crease pulled into the diner parking lot and backed in far from the nearest car. He pulled out a cigarette and lit up, sitting there smoking while the guy watched him, trying to act like stone but the terror flitting across his face in ripples. "What's your name?"

"Cholo."

Cholo. A Spanish word that had come to mean a tough guy, a cowboy. Every third guy coming up from south of the border was called Cholo, and none of them seemed to get the hint that maybe the word was wearing itself out.

"I've never seen you before. Where'd Tucco outsource you from?"

"I run with Jinga's boys, sometimes."

"I'm going to let you off here. Tucco will be along any minute, but keep out of sight."

"Why?"

Asking the question without taking the time to try to piece it together. This one wasn't going to last long.

"Because he'll kill you," Crease said. "Puts the blame on me and he gets to have a little extra fun. He's probably bored and pissed off, him and Cruez taking this long drive up here. Puts him out of sorts."

"They say he's crazy."

"They're right."

"They say you're crazy too."

"They're pretty smart, whoever's giving you all this good information."

Cholo shifted in his seat, looked over at the diner. Never even questioning if what Crease was telling him was the truth. Never thinking Crease might pull the gun again and put one behind his ear the minute he looked away. It was pretty clear why Jinga was such a small-timer, using dummies like this.

"What do I do here?" Cholo asked.

"Nobody in this part of Vermont is going to give you a ride unless you pay for it. A couple hundred bucks and you should be able to make your way back to New York with one of the truckers. Go back to Jinga and pretend this never happened."

"I don't have a couple hundred bucks," Cholo said, sounding embarrassed.

Crease stared at him for a while, thinking this situation was just getting goofier by the minute. "How much was Tucco paying you to take me out?"

"Twenty g's. But only after I did it."

"Way too much money to just ice a guy. Tucco never meant to pay you no matter how it turned out. You always get at least half the cash up front, that's how you know somebody's serious. You get it a couple days in advance so you can spread the word that you got something going on. Then, if anything happens to you, your boys know who to go see."

Cholo's face firmed up and his eyes darkened with understanding. "I never thought of that."

"You might want to try another profession, maybe go back to business school or something." Crease went into his pocket, pulled out two hundred bucks in fifties and stuck them in Cholo's hand, the one that wasn't covered with blood.

5

He got back to Hangtree, found a pay phone, and called Mimi. She answered on the tenth ring and shrieked, "What!"

"It's me," Crease said.

"Why is it you call here and never your own house?"

"You know why."

"I know you shouldn't be afraid of your own wife and son. Is that how you go through your day, worried that you might have to talk to your wife and kid?"

"Ex-wife."

"Only because it's the way you wanted it. And Stevie's not your ex-son, in case you're confused about that."

The kids were yelling in the background and Mimi turned away from the phone to scream.

"How is she?" Crease asked. "How's Joan?"

"Doing her best. Stevie got in trouble at school again. Fighting. He's a bully. He storms around the lunchroom and terrorizes the other kids, even ones who are two, three grades ahead of him. The principal wants to speak to you. He says Stevie would benefit from a father's direct influence. You know what that means? He's talking about the belt. A kid like that, eight years old and punching other kids in the face, he needs a good belting." A dog started to bark. Crease didn't know Mimi had a dog. It sounded small and yippy, the kind that made neighbors go berserk and kill whole families. "I'd like you to talk to Joseph too, when you come around again, if you come around again. He could use a little guidance, a firm lecture. He doesn't listen to me."

"Who?"

"Who what?"

"Who's Joseph? The dog?"

"Joseph, my oldest!" she yelled. "You don't remember? Thirteen, he's got sandy hair, beady eyes. The dog's name is Freddy." Another voice rose, shouting that his eyes weren't beady, they were smoky. Girls at school called them smoky. Mimi shouted back, "Use condoms, always use condoms. They teach you that in sex education yet?"

Crease remembered a beady-eyed little kid, but Christ, now Joey was thirteen, being called Joseph, getting sweet-talked by schoolgirls. Crease shook his head, knowing his old life was further away than maybe it had ever been before.

"She misses you," Mimi said. "I don't know what's been going on with you these last couple of years, or why you're calling me so much, but if it means you're going through a mid-life crisis, then I hope you get over it soon and get the hell back on track. You know what I'm saying?"

He was twenty-seven. If this was a mid-life crisis it didn't say much for his longevity. Still fifty-four was longer than his own father had made it.

"You listening to me, Crease?"

"Yes."

"You've done better by me than my sister. I appreciate it and . . . *shut up in there*! I appreciate it, but you need to think of Joan now. Call her. Deal with your son too. He's only got one father no matter what happens."

Mimi hung up before Crease could say anything else. He stood there with the phone buzzing in his ear, a couple kids riding by on bicycles, a young couple pushing a baby girl in a stroller. If this was any other town, he might think this was a nice place to live.

He looked in the trunk. The steaks were still frozen. He gunned it to Reb's place.

Not much got to him, but he had to admit, watching Reb burn the hell out of the sirloins really started taking its toll. He sat there at her kitchen table, drinking wine, occasionally taking a forkful of salad, but the smoke was making his nose itch. Reb didn't seem to notice the gray haze rising up from the pan while the grease spattered all over. He craned his neck to look into the kitchen.

She flipped the steaks and flipped them again, with the flame up way too high and the meat turning black. He wondered where her head was at, what it is that she was seeing, because she just wasn't picking up on the fact that in about ten more seconds they were going to be eating cereal for dinner instead.

She glanced at him and saw his face and immediately forked the sirloins into two plates. There were some chopped up carrots on the plates alongside potatoes that she'd baked until they were shrunken and wrinkled. It no longer surprised him that she was so skinny.

She put his food in front of him and handed him butter and salt like she knew he was going to need a lot of it to kill the taste. She smiled at him in a pleasant, *Isn't this a nice way to spend the evening* kind of way.

She didn't know how it was done. Joan used to give him the real thing, every night, the perfect homemaker, loving and kind, sweeter with him than he deserved, but somebody he always had to put a front on for. She loved him through all his cynical silence and blamed only herself when he asked for a divorce. It showed him just how off the mark he'd gone. Any other man would be thankful to have a wife like that.

"You aren't eating," Reb said. "Too well-done for you?"

"No," he said, and started cutting into the charred meat.

She sipped her wine and stepped over to the sideboard, got out two candlesticks, placed them on the table, and lit the candles. She sat and began eating and he couldn't figure out why she was trying to get at him this way, acting the part of a lover, attempting to be a spouse, doing things to make her man cozy. He knew he hadn't given her that impression.

"You're going to go to the Burkes' house next, aren't you?" she asked.

"Soon."

"You remember those people?"

"Yes," he said. He'd never spoken to Mary's parents, but he knew their faces. They'd stare at him in town and he'd stare back, his father's iniquity marking him. He knew that no matter how he approached them or what he said, it was bound to be an awful scene. But he couldn't see any way around it.

"You'll never find out what happened," Reb told him. His own thoughts tossed back at him. "Digging it up now will only cause more trouble."

"Maybe not," he said. Suddenly the burned steak didn't taste so bad anymore. It had no taste at all. He finished the meal very quickly and opened a second bottle of wine. It was old cheap stuff, the kind somebody who doesn't really like you gives you for a present over the holidays. It didn't make a difference.

He felt like he was on a stage, being watched by an audience interested in farce, all of them out in the darkness waiting for him to say something funny, to snap off a well-written piece of dialogue.

This was parody. This was burlesque.

"What happens if you find the money?" she asked.

"What do you mean?"

"Who gets it? Who are you supposed to turn it in to? Do the Burkes get it again? I mean, can they prove it's theirs? If you just find a stash?"

He tried to picture Reb laid back across the leather sofa in Tucco's penthouse, with the coke and H spread out on the glass-top table, the wads of cash stacked all over the place. Guys heating spoons and hitting the spike side by side on the U-shaped sectional, watching the Jets on the HD plasma. If she was ever dropped into the middle of that kind of life she'd be dead inside of three months.

Truth was, he didn't know what would happen to the money. If he turned it in, Edwards would probably march off with it. He looked at Reb and saw her mind twirling with the wanting of the fifteen grand. The pulse in her throat was pounding so hard he thought it might break the thin, silver necklace she wore tonight. He wondered what it might be like to care that much about money. About anything.

"I don't know," he said.

That got her dreaming up more ideas. The fire was growing within her. He didn't have the heart to tell her that fifteen k just isn't that much. Why didn't she already know that?

He sat there holding the glass of wine, sipping it and trying to figure what her next move would be. She was already trying to show him that she knew him better than anybody else, that she was inside his head, dirty and sharp as he was. That they were two of a kind.

Maybe it didn't have everything to do with the lost ransom. Maybe she had something else brewing. He tried to picture what it might be, and saw her unfolding a piece of paper across the dining room table and showing him little x's on a map of the town bank. Telling him, *Here's the manager's desk, and here's where the head teller does her transactions . . . only one security guard, an old guy named Edgar . . .*

Reb looked at him and said, "What?"

"Nothing."

"You thinking about your son?"

"Yes," he said.

"You make time for him?"

"Not enough," Crease admitted.

Reb stood, sort of pirouetted around him. She took his hand and led him across the room to the couch. She pressed him down and lay stretched out, half in his lap, her hair strewn across his legs.

"You never loved your wife," she said. "It's pretty clear to me."

"I loved her as well as I could. As I can."

"It's not enough though."

"It is for her, but it shouldn't be. I couldn't do it to her any longer."

"You knew it was going to be like that even when you married her, didn't you?"

"No," he told her. He'd had no idea that the distance between him and Joan would be so great. The distance between him and anyone else, everyone else, except maybe Tucco.

"You think you became a different person along the way?"

He'd thought about that a lot. "No, but you don't know what your strengths and weaknesses are until you're forced to find out."

He could see she wanted to ask him, And what are your strengths? What are your weaknesses? But she was too smart to come right out with it. She wanted to take the time to maneuver things properly. It was fun watching her try to work him.

He knew that as soon as she figured out she wasn't going to get anything from him, she'd toss him out of the house. Maybe even call Edwards and try to incite the sheriff to bust him. Or go back to Jimmy or somebody just like Jimmy and hope to spur him on to take a shot at Crease. You never knew what the next dilemma was going to be or where it was going to come from.

"Now do you want to go to bed?" she asked.

Crease let out a grin. It was starting to feel like New York around here.

6

Wildlife had overtaken the old mill. The log ramps and tramcar flatbeds where the rough-cut lumber used to be loaded were covered over by tall grass, weeds, and saplings. He walked around the mill. There were broken floorboards everywhere. The roof had collapsed from heavy winter snows over the last four decades, and the rotted timbers lay crossing each other in heaps. Daylight shined in, and there were animal nests and signs of teenage vandalism everywhere.

Crease tried to piece together the events of that night, the way his father had laid them out. Old rusted steam-powered saws and other machinery still lay about in the long, wide main room.

His father would have been behind one of the trimmers, where the carriages worked back and forth ripping through the grain. There was a man-sized open area between two of them where a man could stretch out. From there he would be able to see the front door, down the length of the factory floor, and also keep his back mostly protected.

Crease looked around and found where his father most likely hid the cash. Probably inside the rusted metal spoked wheels where the cut slabs were placed on flatbeds reeled down the slope by cables out the back of the mill. It was an incline system, typical of the way things were done in the '30s and '40s. The wheels were overhead but close enough.

Crease had seen fifteen grand in tens and twenties before. It didn't look like much. A couple of stacks a few inches high. He acted out taking the bundles of cash from the satchel and placing the money beneath the flatbed.

The mill was a good spot for the kidnappers to make the trade. No way for an ambush to work. Plenty of exits. Line of sight was fifty yards to the tree line in any direction. There were logging trails all up and down the hills. They could shake anybody chasing them.

If his father had seen Edwards in the tree line, then the kidnappers would've seen him too. Edwards had botched any chance of a straight switch.

Crease took up the position for a long wait, glancing about every so often across the width of the factory. Checking behind him, filling his head with his father's thoughts. He tried to imagine that fifteen thousand would be worth everything in the world, paying off the damn doctors. It would settle bad debts, allow for some breathing room with the mortgage company. What else? Not even a new car. A nicer secondhand model maybe. A couple rounds of drinks at the bar. Crease just couldn't understand it.

Still, he decided to ride it out. He imagined the door opening wide, the silhouette of a man with a gun in his hand. Crease held his arm out and fired twice. He would've put the guy down, but his father had missed.

His old man had been too keyed up. He said he'd waited in the mill from noon on. Four hours, five, six. Only tipping back some whiskey from a flask every now and again. It wouldn't have lasted long. After a couple of hours, he'd have had the shakes. He would've tried to get away from the pain. He might've slept.

Crease got back in position between the trimmers. He ran through it again. Saw how the guy at the door would be firing back. Turned and looked for bullet holes in the machinery near him. There weren't any. Up higher, near the log ramp. He found a ricochet mark that had scored and twisted one of the wheels on another flatbed. The bullet would've gone right out the platform opening where they hauled down the lumber. It proved Edwards hadn't hit the girl.

Now he had an idea of what the scene was like. He imagined Mary Burke wandering through. Which direction would she come from? The far end of the factory. The 'nappers spotted Edwards in the woods, didn't want to come in the front door, and sneaked in through the other side where the rough-cut lumber would be loaded on the log ramps. His father was so worried about Edwards stealing the money that he hadn't been paying enough attention to all the other ways the 'nappers might get inside. They could've been in there before him, waiting him out, watching him suck down his booze and fade into sleep. Then they tippy-toed to where the cash was hidden and plucked it out while his old man snored on the floor.

So they let the girl go. Six years old. Maybe they'd told her to just walk straight ahead, the nice sheriff would take her home to her mommy and daddy. She walks forward, stroking her teddy bear's head, probably talking to it the way Stevie used to talk to his. We're going home now, Teddy.

The fever broke inside Crease.

It happened so suddenly that he didn't know why there was the sound of twisting metal until he looked down at his hands. He'd gripped the edge of the trimmer and was pulling on the heavy iron sidebar of it, wrenching it loose. He tasted blood and realized he'd bitten his tongue. Sweat ran down his face and snaked across his scalp. In less than a minute he was so wet it looked as if a hose had been turned on him.

His father aiming at Edwards. The deputy's revolver going off, and now, the little girl walking past. He could almost see his father turning the gun on her, firing while thinking, No witnesses.

All of it such a waste. The girl snuffed for nothing. His father's downfall completed. The 'nappers didn't even make enough money to change their lives any. Why had they only asked for fifteen k? What could you buy that would make this all worth it? Christ, it wasn't even a big enough bump in somebody's bank account for anyone else to notice. Not like somebody who walks off with a million bucks. Those assholes you could spot easily, some lowlife buying a Cadillac for cash.

Crease looked down and saw Mary Burke dead on the floor.

We're going home now, Teddy.

The house gave off the same vibe as a lot of the others in town. A second rate effort had been made to fix the place up within the last few years. A new coat of paint had been added, but the paint was cheap and the job had been sloppy. The foundation had been reset with brick, but the brickwork hadn't been perfect and the rain and snow wash had already made it partially topple. Hedge roses had been planted along the front edge of the property to give it some curb appeal. They were overgrown and choking each other.

Crease stood on Sheriff Edwards' porch and knocked on the door.

Edwards answered in a stained tee-shirt and torn trousers, barefoot. His wet, bloated features, especially the busted schnoz weaving across his face, were even more unsettling now that he was out of uniform. He really did look like Crease's old man. Jesus.

The sheriff stood there and said, "You. Rebecca Fortlow's friend, so you said. You're at my house? You come to my house?"

"I came to your house," Crease said.

"Who the hell do you think you are coming to my house? Standing here on my doorstep. What do you want here? You got a problem? Don't bring it here."

Clearly Edwards' concept of civic duty ended the minute he clocked out. "I'd like to talk to you."

"How'd you know where I live? You following me?"

"I've always known where you lived."

"What the hell's that mean? I ought to book you for trespassing. Don't you move. I've got some questions for you."

"I've got a few for you too."

Edwards reached out to grab Crease's jacket. The hands were slow, even slower than Jimmy Devlin's.

Look at them having to struggle through the air, so fat and weak. He was so soft now that his body wobbled behind the arms, left to right, sorta *chugunga chugunga.* Crease still couldn't quite believe this was the same guy that had stirred so much inside of him when he was a kid. The hands still coming.

Crease turned and sidestepped, and Edwards' arms shot past him. Crease thought how easy it would be to yank the Bowie, bring it up easy, without even any real force, and snap it under Edwards' chin, jam it into his brain. Sometimes you couldn't think too hard on a thing, your body might respond before you decided you were just joking.

"Get in here!"

Give him his moment. What the hell. It was where Crease wanted to go anyway. He slipped inside and let Edwards shove him from behind. Once, twice. Again. Edwards was out of breath already, the air hissing from the sides of his mouth.

The living room was small, fairly clean, devoid of a woman's touch. A greasy bag stood open on the coffee table and a couple of hamburgers from a fast food joint sat unwrapped on it. There was one full beer bottle on the table, four empty ones, and a half-finished pint of Dewars. A .38 Smith & Wesson revolver sat on the mantel, wedged between a couple of frames of middle-aged women posing in mock cheesecake.

There were a lot of photos of Edwards and different women all over the place. The same lady never popped up twice. What did that tell you about the sheriff? Usually it was embarrassing not to latch on to one that was worth your while, but Edwards was showing off the fact. Declaring to everybody—even the women—that this is just routine, this has happened many times before, this means nothing. You weren't supposed to be looking at the ladies, you were meant to keep your eyes on him.

Crease knew he was the reason why. It was because Edwards was no longer beautiful. His pettiness and fury came from a whole different place now than it did back in the days when he'd torment Crease and his father. Now, every morning Edwards had to wake up and look in the mirror and see a guy he wasn't supposed to be.

"What do you want?" Edwards asked.

"Answers."

"You're going to talk to me, kid, or I'm going to put you away."

"I am talking to you."

Edwards pulled a face. What Joan used to call a boo-boo face when Stevie got upset and pouty. It wasn't a good look on a fat, pissy alcoholic. Edwards glanced around the room. Crease knew he was looking for his gun, but he'd forgotten where he'd left it. There was plenty of time. Crease could walk over there and pick it up, hand it to him. Instead he just stood there, waiting. Eventually Edwards spotted it, stormed over, and plucked it up.

Edwards pointed the S&W .38 at Crease, holding it in his right hand. Crease wasn't sure if the guy was just paranoid or if he really did have fine-tuned instincts and could sense one of his victims rising up before him. Crease wondered what the sheriff might be expecting. Tears? Drop to the knees?

Crease lit a cigarette. "Well?"

"You son of a bitch. I'm taking you in."

"Taking me in?"

"You heard me."

"On what charge?"

"I'll worry about that later."

"I think you should worry about it now."

"I'll worry about it later!"

"I just want to talk."

"I don't give a damn. You listen to me. We're going to move slow." Edwards was in cop mode, which didn't bear any resemblance to the cop mode Crease knew. "You're going to walk backwards to me. Turn in the hall. Then walk out to the driveway and get in the back of my cruiser. You're going to talk to me downtown or I'm—"

Crease let the cigarette dangle from the corner of his mouth. It was something his father used to do before the big fall. It gave his old man a cool '50s hipster look. Crease wasn't sure what it did for him, but he needed his hands free, while Edwards was throwing around the tough talk.

He moved.

His left forearm shot out and snapped hard against the inside of Edwards' right wrist, shoving the gun away. Crease's right hand flashed out and his palm thrust under Edwards' chin, shoving him up onto his tippy-toes. Then his fingers clenched into the sides of the sheriff's jaw. It was a good hold, one that Cruez had taught him. You didn't even have to hurt the guy, just lift and grab and the whole body went along. Edwards' eyes filled with panic.

Crease gripped the sheriff's gun hand and tightened his fingers on the nerve center in the wrist. Edwards held on and Crease kept tightening his grip, slowly putting on more pressure. Edwards' hand went dead and flopped open, the .38 balancing there on his palm like he was making an offering. Crease closed his hand into a fist and slugged Edwards twice across the bridge of his nose.

It was enough. The gun fell on the floor and the sheriff dropped to his knees, blood running from his nose and mouth.

The women all over the place looked down at him. Crease picked up the S&W and put it in his pocket. Then he helped Edwards to his feet and walked him over to his lounge chair and sat him down. Crease cranked back the lever and put the sheriff's feet up on the foot rest, got him nice and comfortable. Crease sat on the coffee table, facing him, still smoking the cigarette.

He'd thought that getting his hands on Edwards again after all these years would have a greater meaning for him. Siphon off some of the fever, put his old man's ghost back to sleep. Give him some kind of a perk, make him boil with laughter, fill him with joy. At least give him a chuckle.

But Crease felt nothing but a little pity for the guy and a concern about whether he was making all the wrong moves for all the wrong reasons.

He looked a little closer at the sheriff now. He saw that Edwards had a fairly recent knife wound on his forearm and buckshot scars across his shoulder, a few pings to the neck. The top half of one of his ears was gone and the cartilage ended in a ragged kink. Somebody's teeth had done it. If nothing else, the sheriff was the real deal, for Vermont. He'd gotten roughed up on the job.

"Who are you?" Edwards asked. "What do you want here in my town? In my house? You're asking for a lot of hurt, kid."

You had to, if you were going to get anywhere.

Crease said, "Tell me why you didn't come clean about Mary Burke."

Edwards' eyes focused but the blood kept dribbling from his nose and across his white tee-shirt. Once your nose was broken it didn't take much to crack it again. Crease found a mustard-smeared napkin near the burgers and tossed it to Edwards. The sheriff tore it in half, balled each piece and gently eased them into his nostrils.

"I didn't hit you that hard," Crease said.

"Broken capillaries. I get nosebleeds easy." Edwards was trying to play it cool, roll along with the set-up. It was the smart move to make, and the fact that he made it surprised Crease. "Give me my beer."

Crease handed it to him. "Listen—"

"And the whiskey."

"Listen—"

"Son, you've just bought yourself a whole world of trouble."

"I think you should listen—"

"Striking an officer of the law. You can do two years for that."

Cool but not cool enough. Now he was going to rag talk. You can't spook a guy who's taken your gun away. "You never were very smart."

The voice, in the quiet of the house, came on strong and resonant and ancient. Edwards might remember now. The afternoon of the funeral, the days afterward in the jail kicking the crap out of Crease. Edwards' gray matter had gone through a lot, but certain memories would be seared in there good. Crease finished his cigarette. Edwards' expression suddenly smoothed and his eyes flooded with recognition.

Crease thought, Here we go.

"You. You! You're back!"

"I'm back."

Edwards couldn't control himself. He shot up out of the chair and lunged at Crease, letting out a growl. He hurtled forward, his gut leading the way. He caught Crease around the waist, lifted him off the table, and carried him three steps across the room. The women smiled blankly, watching the scene. Crease spotted one he recognized. It was Reb.

Reb's had enough problems without all you boys chasing her farther off the narrow path.

He let out a sigh just before he was driven into the far wall. A paint-by-numbers of Jesus on a cloud with his arms open swung crazily beside him. A picture of a dog fell to the floor and broke into a hundred pieces. Crease saw it was a jigsaw puzzle that had been glued together and hung up.

Somehow, the very thought of it got the fever going inside him again. Not his past humiliation, his anger, not even his father's death. It had nothing to do with the man's cruelty. For some reason, it was the goddamn dog.

"Okay," Crease said.

His hands flashed out and plucked the wadded up bits of napkin out of Edwards' nostrils. His fists, almost on their own accord, rapped Edwards twice in the nose until blood burst and arced across the floor. Crease worked slowly, expertly, chopping the sheriff in the throat, driving a knee into his thigh, jabbing, striking him in the solar plexus. It was slow, methodical work, just like Edwards had given him back in the jail cell.

Thinking of the man putting the puzzle together, carefully like a child, working with the glue, and taking the time to hang it on the wall. Probably stepping back to view it with a certain kind of pride, even love. It was taunting as hell, thinking of the guy like that. An affront to his senses.

All of these years adding up to so little, but the dog, man, the dog. That was insulting, that was something he couldn't suffer.

He held his fist high for one more strike, but Edwards was nearly out cold on his feet. It took all of ten seconds. The paint-by-numbers Jesus was still swaying. Crease took the sheriff in his arms and duck-walked him back to his chair. Got him settled, got his feet up again.

He went to the kitchen and found more napkins and a dish towel. He wet them and returned to Edwards, who was moaning the way Crease's father used to moan in the gutter after the whores had thrown him out on the street.

This damn town, he couldn't do anything without thinking of the old man.

Crease started to wash the blood from the sheriff's face. He checked the nose. It wasn't broken this time, but kept on bleeding. He got more napkin up in there. Pressed the cold towel to the Edwards' forehead, wet down his neck. The sheriff quit moaning and started to snore. Crease sat back on the coffee table and lit another cigarette.

A part of him very much wanted to clean up the jigsaw pieces. He thought maybe he was losing some of his edge in Hangtree.

Edwards was enjoying his nap. He cooed like a baby. It took a while for him to wake up.

Crease said, "I'm on the job. You're not about to bully me. You want to file charges, you do it. You want to come at me some other way, that's fine too. But that's for later. Right now I want to know about Mary Burke. You were there the day of the switch."

For a second it looked like Edwards might try to muscle his way through, like he was going to dive across the room again. But then he shifted, grunted in pain, visibly deflated and sank back in the chair.

He said, "I was there. The switch never happened."

"You were going to pull a job and grab the cash. You were staked out in the woods, keeping an eye on my old man. You were both dirty and had the same idea to bounce the fifteen grand."

Edwards said nothing.

"My father hid the cash in the mill. Somebody cut the girl loose and plucked the money, probably while he was dozing or too drunk to notice. You got impatient after all those hours and showed at the door. You both tried to ice each other and the girl got it instead."

"I didn't want to kill him. I—"

The way he said it got Crease curious. "What?"

Edwards had some trouble getting it out. He tried to sit up in the chair but he hurt too much. He let out another groan through his clenched teeth. Whatever he was about to say was coming up from down deep.

"What?" Crease repeated.

"He taught me everything! He was my friend! Don't you know that? Don't you see that, you shit? My mentor." Edwards' feet bounced against the foot rest like an angry child's. "I wasn't there to steal the money, I was looking out for him! I knew what he was planning. I could see it in his eyes, the way he was walking around the office. I didn't want him to make the worst mistake of his life. Fifteen g's, it was nothing. All he had to do was lay off the sauce and get himself organized. But he was too drunk most of the time. He wouldn't listen to me, couldn't see the only way to get out was to step up and clean up. It was easier for him to hatch a stupid plan on the spur of the moment. He snatched the money and was too wasted to even cover his zone. I walked in to check on him and he got off one shot and killed Mary Burke. I thought he was ready to shoot me too, to cover it up, and I fired a warning shot over his head just to settle him down, get that fucking notion right out of his head."

Crease looked away. He spied the dog in pieces again. All those years of torment because Edwards felt angry and ashamed at being let down by the old man. In a way they were brothers. Jesus.

"I don't know what happened to that money," the sheriff said. "Nobody does."

"Somebody does," Crease said.

"So that's what you want?" Edwards let his smile out, showing off all those teeth again. It was still the movie star's leer, he hadn't lost that. His voice was starting to go out, weak from Crease having jabbed him in the throat. He swallowed more beer. "That fifteen grand? Just like your father."

You think of a little six-year-old girl and you can't imagine that a bullet could get inside that tiny body and actually fragment into even smaller pieces. Fact is, a little kid, with soft bones, the bullet races around ricocheting for a while until the kid's cut apart and there's hardly anything left of the slug.

We're not going home, Teddy. We're never going home again.

Crease felt his blood rushing even as his face broke out in sweat. In seconds his hair was dripping and he had to mop his brow and upper lip. He started to pant and the moisture ran down his neck.

Edwards said, "What the hell is wrong with you? You sick? Have a bite of whiskey."

"Shh. Let's not get distracted. Who were your suspects?"

"We only had one. Your father."

Crease sat back and lit another cigarette. "He didn't do it."

"I'm still not so sure about that."

"I am. He wanted the cash but he didn't score the girl. It just fell into his lap." Crease let out a trail of smoke, looking up at Reb on the in the photo, smiling and looking happy, holding Edwards' hand. They made a good couple. "Family enemies?"

"None."

"Business partner who wanted to cash out but couldn't?"

"Burke ran the hardware store. Still does. No partners. No unhappy ex-employees. We did our job. I did my job."

"Background checks on the family?"

"You're not listening to me. We did our jobs. There were no outstanding debts. Wife didn't have a boyfriend who might want easy rent off the husband." The sheriff's expression became a bit more sure and arrogant. "And it wasn't me."

His chin was up, dignified, daring Crease to judge him. Not knowing that Crease was a bent cop himself, and had seen a lot of his brothers in blue pocket a hell of a lot more than fifteen g's. It almost made him laugh.

He began to cool down. He lit another butt.

"What time did the 'nappers say they'd do the trade?"

"They said to get there by one p.m. and wait. Your father said he'd handle it alone, didn't want to endanger the girl." Edwards couldn't help scowling. "Didn't want any backup. If you're really on the job you know that breaks every rule there is."

Crease knew it all right. "What made you bust into the mill when you did? My father said six hours went by. Why'd you get up right then?"

"It was closer to four. He got there late. He told everybody he arrived at the mill at noon, but it was after one, he'd already missed the chance to get any kind of a drop. He stopped at a liquor store first to load up, left the satchel full of money that Burke had given him right in the passenger seat. I had a bad feeling right from the beginning and I was watching him."

Edwards began to tremble and Crease handed him the Dewars to help calm his nerves. All of this rage, and Edwards was a near carbon copy of Crease's old man. He watched the sheriff take a good bite, saw his eyes roll up in pleasure and relief. Edwards let out a deeply satisfied, nearly carnal sigh, the same way Crease's father used to do it.

"It was getting dark. I had parked back on one of the trails and left my flashlight in the car. I wanted to make an on-site evaluation of the situation. Make sure your old man hadn't passed out, check and see if the kidnappers had already slipped away."

"You didn't want him to blow the collar."

"That's right. I wanted the girl back. I didn't want him to botch the set-up and ruin his life. But he did."

Crease couldn't get back into that now. He needed clarity. "Why'd you walk in the front door? That seems stupid to me."

"The sun was to my back. I wanted anybody in the mill to be blind. I wanted the perp but I didn't want to get shot for it. By the 'nappers or your old man."

"Why didn't either of you see the girl until the last second?"

Edwards had nothing to say to that. His expression twisted again. Crease understood why he would've blamed his father entirely for everything that happened. The missed opportunity, the screwy rendezvous, the dead girl. His mentor had let him down. He was green, and he'd done the right thing the wrong way.

"You're not going to solve this," Edwards told him.

"Would you want me to?" Crease asked.

"Hell yes, clear the books for me. But this one's long gone, and your father was a part of it."

"You too."

"Only because I couldn't save her."

He knew Edwards was right.

He'd never get to the end of it. He'd run around town chasing his tail, like he did when he was a kid. It was a holding pattern. He wasn't a gold shield detective, had never worked homicide. He could trip over the 'nappers five times in an afternoon and wouldn't know it.

"Okay," Crease said, and that was the end of it for now.

Only Edwards didn't think so. He said, "Fair warning, kid. You and me still have business."

"All right."

"I don't care if you are on the job. You're not getting away with this, treating me like this in my own home." Crease half-expected him to say, *Messing with my jigsaw dog!* "I owe you. There's no way you're walking away from this now. It's going to catch up with you. Maybe not today or tomorrow, but soon."

Crease reached into his pocket, handed Edwards back his gun, and said, "Why wait?"

He sat there within arm's reach thinking of how many ways he could kill the sheriff before the guy got a shot off.

Crease could use the knife he'd pulled off Jimmy, or the butterfly blade he'd taken from the foul-up Tucco hired. Or he could draw his own .38. These podunks would never be able to match the bullet to him. Or he could just reach out with his hands and squeeze Edwards' neck until the man turned purple and blue and then black.

He waited, all these scenes of murder running through his mind. And he wasn't even mad at the guy anymore.

Edwards just sat there, his mouth open, napkins up his nose.

Eventually Crease got bored, stubbed the butt on the corner of the coffee table, stood and got out of there.

7

The Bentley with tinted windows started following him as he turned the corner onto Main Street. It wasn't exactly an undercover vehicle. A few cars were around, some foot traffic on the sidewalks, shopkeepers out front. It was as good a place as any to get the next bit of business out of the way. He pulled the 'Stang over, climbed out, and leaned against it while the Bentley drew up behind him and parked.

Cruez lumbered out of the driver's side. He went six-seven, a man-monster weighing maybe three-fifty, with a face like a lump of clay that a class of emotionally disturbed children had pounded the hell out of. He liked using a .357 long-barrel Magnum. In his hand, it looked like a derringer.

Cruez had saved Crease's life twice and Crease had returned the favor a couple of times during bad double-cross deals over the years. Crease knew their shared history wouldn't stop the monolith for a second if Tucco gave the word. Cruez was an insanely loyal dog to his master. All the bosses had a guy like this. He was imposing enough to keep away the minor troublemakers, rough enough to do damage when he had to, and huge enough that he could block a few bullets while the big cheese ran for cover.

This was going to be a scene.

Tucco was already drawing it out, taking his time getting out of the Bentley. Showing Crease that nobody could ever get away, he'd follow you down any rabbit hole, even if it led to Vermont. Cruez stood at the back door of the Bentley, opened it, and waited.

The seconds ticked off. Crease didn't feel like watching. He very much wanted to see Morena and was afraid the weakness was showing in his face. He was out of cigarettes so he stepped up the curb to a nearby convenience store and asked for his brand. They were out. He asked for another. They'd never heard of them. Finally he just pointed to a pack and paid.

Cruez was in the same spot, the back door of the Bentley still open, Tucco still inside with Morena. Man, the drama. Where the hell would any of them be without the drama. All of this and nothing was going to happen today anyway. This was just the second push.

Finally Tucco slid free from the car. Today he was dressed like a Wall Street stockbroker in a four thousand dollar black suit, long leather coat tugged to the side so you could see the suit, nice shades. He and Cruez and the car looked as out of place in Hangtree as they might've in the Mississippi Delta.

Tucco stood 5'3, going about a hundred-thirty pounds of bone and wiry sinew. He had a slight Spanish accent that he consciously affected so he could sound like a Spanish Harlem tough. Otherwise he sounded as uptown as anybody in a white collar. Truth was, he'd been hand-fed by maids and grown up with a view of Museum Mile in Manhattan, the son of two highly successful stockbrokers who made their biggest hauls every time the economy took a downturn. They raked it in during the Reagan years. Tucco had built up his double-life from scratch, same as Crease had.

It wasn't an act anymore. When Tucco gave the dead gaze it would rattle almost anybody. The lifelessness there, the pure infinite blackness of it. Crease had never been able to figure out where it came from. Not poverty, not shame. Not even rage over real or imagined slights. Crease had talked to Tucco stoned, sated, and medicated in the hospital with his guts opened up to drain. Tucco had rambled and whispered and hissed and Crease still didn't know a thing about what really went on behind the guy's eyes.

You could push Tucco pretty hard. He liked it, going right to the edge. Crease had seen it several times while they worked together. How the traffickers would talk circles around him and rip him off right in front of his eyes, and Tucco wouldn't do anything about it. The other dealers, especially the Colombians and Haitians, they'd chop a guy to pieces with a machete if he spoke out of turn or stepped on someone's shoe.

But Tucco liked walking the rim of his own malevolence. Sometimes for weeks or months, until the day came when someone would go too far, and Tucco would finally have enough. He'd react fast as a serpent then, pulling the butterfly blade and going to work with it. Sometimes it would be over fast and sometimes he really took his time.

He'd make the gang watch. Guys with ten kills who were hard as iron would turn green and pass out. Tucco liked to turn and give a grin to Crease, and Crease would light another cigarette and grin back. He'd put it all down in his reports, every detail no matter how insane or unbelievable it sounded, and the squad would go and bust some other honcho. No matter what he did, nobody wanted Tucco badly enough to let Crease drag him in.

Tucco stepped up, took one look around Main Street, and said, "No wonder you got a taste for the life, coming from a hole like this."

"Yeah."

"How long were you here?"

"Until I was seventeen."

"That explains why you're crazy."

The life didn't just mean money and slick cars and strutting into a booked restaurant without a reservation and getting the best table. It was the darkness, the dirty belly, the fear in the other guy's eyes, the being bad, and the knowledge that you could take whatever you wanted so long as you could keep it.

Crease said, "Anybody can get a taste for the life. Look at you. You like to play that you come from Spanish Harlem, but your parents were top line shakers and you were born on Fifth Avenue. Not in the back of a cab either. When you were a baby, you had servants trading off diapering you. If you were lucky, your mother maybe changed you on Sundays."

"Nah, she'd just make me hold out until Monday, when the maid came back to work. It was all right."

"You like the ride up here?"

"Yeah. I like the trees. All the colors, this is the right time of the year to catch them. I'd heard about people doing that, caravans of cars coming up this way, mooks driving three hundred miles just to stare at the leaves. It always sounded really stupid to me. But I liked it. What else they got up here? Syrup?"

"Yeah," Crease said. "There's syrup. And military boarding schools. Bed and breakfasts. Dairy farms. Lots of them."

"That just about it?"

"And llamas."

Tucco drew his chin back, his shades reflecting Crease's face back at him. "What?"

"Yeah."

"C'mon. The hell for?"

"Special wool for bulky sweaters."

"Is that right?"

It was a dumb conversation, but you always had to have dumb conversations with the other guy when both of you were waiting for the other to jump first. A part of your head was anticipating the knife, thinking about how long it would take you to get out your own. Meanwhile, you talked about leaves and llamas.

Cruez was just standing there looking like one of Zapata's banditos. You could hack at his face with an ax and probably not notice the difference afterward. He didn't worry Crease, but he might get in the way just enough to trip him up.

Tucco took off the shades. He wanted to show off the death glare, try to really spook the shit out of Crease. It wasn't going to work but you had to go through these little games, it was just the way that they had to be.

Those black, blank eyes focused on Crease now, Tucco's face empty of all emotion.

"You want to know what I did to her after you left?" Tucco asked. His voice was utterly empty, meaning it was supposed to be serious. But Crease knew he was really laughing inside, still making his own fun.

"I already know," Crease said.

"I cut her." Tucco tried to smile and his lips barely quivered. "I took her nose first. It happened so fast she didn't even know it was gone for a minute. There was nothing but a hole there and I could look all the way back into her head. You think you'd still want to fuck her without a nose? I don't think so. I think you'd throw up. Then I hacked off a few of her fingers. Not too many, just a couple. I left her her thumbs, so she can still open bottles of beer and shit. But they were important to me, those fingers, right? You know what I mean. I didn't like that she'd been touching you with them."

Crease said, "You didn't do anything to her."

"I slit her tongue up the middle, turned her into a snake. Kinda sexy really, I think I'm starting to get a little kinky in my old age, the two pieces slithering around in her mouth. Last, I took her eyes. Those gorgeous eyes, man, and you know I'm someone who appreciates a woman's eyes. The way they twinkle, the way a sexed-up mama gives you that hooded lid look, right, when she's trying to get you into bed. I still got 'em, in a little jar back at home, if you want to see them. Sitting there, the cook serving me, I have the jar next to me, tell it how my day went."

Crease gestured to the Bentley. "You left your window open."

"What?"

"I can see her in the back seat drinking, looks like a scotch on the rocks. Not that I'd ever believe you'd hurt her. Not even if her fingers did touch me."

Tucco turned and looked back at the car, tilted his head a little to see Morena in the back staring at them, sipping her drink. It was funny and it wasn't funny. She caught Crease's eye and the old familiar ache climbed back into his chest.

Tucco said, "Yeah." His hands started to move. "I'm gonna reach into my pocket for a cigarette."

"No," Crease said. "You're not." Instead, Crease drew his own pack and proffered it.

"What's this? Are those . . . Jesus Christ, are those *menthol*?"

"All the store had left."

Tucco waved them away. "You're making me sad, seeing you like this. How'd this happen to you?"

It was a good question, Crease thought. He still wasn't any closer to an answer.

"You in this place, I'm finding it hard to believe."

"I do too."

The smell of burning leaves drifted through the air. Tucco stared off at the hills in the horizon. "So where'd you bury that other one I sent after you?"

"Jinga's boy? I sent him home."

"You did? How'd he get there?"

"I gave him some cash to pay his way on a truck."

It tickled Tucco so much that he almost let out a laugh. You couldn't ask for more from him. Just seeing a flash of his teeth was like outright hysteria in anybody else. "If Jinga hears that story he'll kill the idiot himself. And you know the imbecile is gonna tell him."

"Seriously, you offered him twenty g's to ice me? You couldn't keep it even slightly realistic?"

"He was a moron to believe me. That Jinga, he hires some stupid people. Not my fault that these dimwits expect every fairy tale you tell them to come true. Besides, I knew he wouldn't get the drop on you. I didn't want him to."

That sounded like the truth. This whole thing, it was just Tucco—and Crease too, he had to admit it—having more fun while they both ramped themselves up, got the adrenaline going. You couldn't take things too seriously in the life, not even while somebody was getting waxed in front of you. While machine guns stitched the walls around you and you hid behind an end table no thicker than cardboard. You always had to take it easy, find the humor in the moment, even if there was none.

"You need much longer to do what you came here to do?" Tucco asked.

"I don't know."

That was an affront. It was squirrelly, not giving an answer. It made Tucco purse his lips and go, "Humph."

Crease lit one of the menthols and took a drag. Jesus, it was like smoking cough drops. "Another couple of days, nothing you can't deal with. Watch the leaves for a while longer. Maybe you can figure out a way to break new territory up here, get some guys in the truck stop to work for you. Get some kickback with smuggling over the border."

"Canada, yeah. Big thing now is wetbacks coming up from south of the border, and Asians coming in from north of the border. Getting guys with 18-wheelers, hauling freight . . . plenty of room for fifty, sixty chinks trying to start a new life."

"See, you can be benevolent. Asians will be naming their kids after you. Tucco Lee."

Tucco's brow started to knot at the thought of it, until he realized Crease was just fucking with him. "So, this thing you have to do here. It has to do with your father? And how you came down to New York, and why you're a narc?"

"In a way, yeah."

"Good, get it squared, then we'll square up, see where we stand."

Crease said, "I'm going to get in the back of the Bentley and talk with her. Give us some privacy."

Tucco was too slick to show he was pissed about it. It went back to how he liked to be pushed right to the edge.

But Cruez swung out in front of Crease and tried to block him, which was the totally wrong move to make. He'd juked the show. Tucco was playing it so cool, and now he had to extend that cool to Cruez too. You could see it got under Tucco's skin a little, having to go the extra yard and put his arm on the monolith and ease him back. It put too much attention on the scene and too much focus on the fact that Crease was getting what he wanted.

Tucco said, "Sure, you get yourself a drink too, all right? Got everything you could want back there." Knowing Crease didn't drink but making the offer anyway. "Your old man, he liked whiskey, right?"

"The cheaper the better." Grinning, Crease let the cigarette dangle. When you had a pose you liked to hit you had to stick with it. "This will only take a minute."

"Take your time in my car, with my woman, man. What's mine is yours."

There was a time when it was true. Tucco wouldn't deny Crease anything. It was part of the action, dangling everything you owned in front of your crew's faces. See which one of them would leap for the bait, which ones wouldn't.

The ones that wouldn't were more greedy. They were only biding their time until they could get it all. The ones who acted like they didn't want anything, those you got rid of first.

8

Crease got in the back of the Bentley and rolled the window up. He turned and Morena was sitting there with the glass in her hand, tinkling ice cubes. First thing he wanted to tell her was that she shouldn't be drinking now that she was pregnant. It sounded ludicrous even to himself.

She said, "I don't know what to call you."

She'd known him by the other name. He'd had that name for the last two and a half years, up until only a few days ago, but he couldn't remember what it was now.

He said, "My name is Crease."

He wondered what would happen next. If she'd throw the drink in his face, slap him, or sidle into his arms. And how he'd react. He wasn't sure what he wanted to do. Kiss her, clasp her hand, press a palm to her belly, start going *kitchy-kitchy coo, kitchy coo.*

Instead, he did nothing and she took another sip and looked at him from beneath the waves of her luminous black hair.

"You're crazier than he is, Crease," she said. "Two years undercover, playing both sides, working me. I've seen you in action. You're clever, crafty, and you thrill to kill. You've got that same glacier gaze when you want it."

"I didn't work you," Crease told her, though he knew he had, even without fully realizing it. "And I only played both sides because that's the way they wanted it."

"You weren't faking. What you were doing, it was all real."

"Yeah."

"You're as bad a boy as any of them."

"You going to lecture me?" he asked. It was probably what attracted her to him in the first place.

She put the glass down and said, "Did you ever care about me? Or was I just a way to get to him?"

"You never gave me anything I could use in court, Morena. They never wanted to bring him up anyway. He's safer than a priest who spits on the sidewalk. I fell for you the first day I saw you."

"All you had to do was ask him. He would've given me to you."

He hated when she talked like that. Laying it on the line, letting the jealousy twist inside him. Reminding him that she used to be on the street before Tucco made her his lady, and then she was a kept woman anyhow. She liked to torment him a little that way, get him riled, charged up, before they hit the bed.

"I wasn't about to ask anybody for you," he said.

She started to move to him but he couldn't help himself any longer and lunged, carried her to the far side of the Bentley where she smacked up against the bar. Bottles rattled and rang. His mouth found hers, but he couldn't swallow her down fast enough or breathe her in deeply enough, and when he grabbed her she let out a cry of pain and amusement. He backed off, afraid of hurting the kid. His son Stevie was eight years old and already a victim of his growing fever, but somehow Crease felt like this one, born into a world of murder and betrayal, had a better chance. How sick was that?

She was right, they were all right, he really was crazy.

He said, "You shouldn't have come."

"Why not? This is where everybody else is. This is where it's all happening. Why should I miss out?" The corners of her mouth were crimped with anger. Her dark eyes blazed, her luxurious nightshade hair wreathed to frame her face. "Why did you do it?" she asked. "Why did you leave like that?"

Perhaps his eyes were full of intense, unclear emotion, the way his father's had been the night he died, because she had to glance away. Crease's thoughts raced but no words formed, nothing came to him. This was his chance to explain, but there was just nothing there.

Finally he said, "I don't know."

"You don't know? That's it? You don't know?"

"Yeah."

And he didn't, but he had to admit he hadn't been asking himself the question. He really didn't care much anymore, which seemed to put things in perspective. The not caring. The understanding that what he was doing made no sense to anyone, not even himself, and yet it was the only thing that could be done.

She must've realized that because she let it slide by. You did weird things. You lived a strange life. She said, "I've missed you."

"You say that like you haven't seen me in ten years. It's been half a week."

"It feels longer."

He nodded. He stared at her and thought of the last time they'd been together, in Tucco's penthouse apartment in Tribeca, looking out over the water. They'd just finished making love and he'd slipped into that zone where he was tired and content and wanted to go out and do something stupid and touristy like taking in a Broadway show. The feeling hit him rarely and always while Morena's scent was still on him.

Morena had been in the bathroom a long time, and just when he was about to get up and go check on her she came out naked holding a home pregnancy test. She cocked an eyebrow and said, "You're a daddy."

He believed her. She never hid behind a line or a rap. She was herself and never played any games. So far as he knew, she'd never told a lie to him or even to Tucco. She always threw it out there and if you didn't like it, the trouble was yours.

So if she said the kid was his, it was his.

A sense of elation began to surge through his chest for a moment before quickly dissipating. He had a son and four or five or six adopted kids, and now there was another on the way. He expected her to run over and show him the test, parading the tiny blue line in front of him the way Joan had, clutching the little piss-soaked stick of plastic to her chest. But Morena had already thrown it in the wastebasket next to the bed, and Crease didn't have the heart to check for himself, go digging around in the trash for it.

A residue of her dried sweat powdered her body as she moved to him across Tucco's bed, and as she touched him he turned to her and pressed his lips to the spot under her ear which made her purr and said, "I'm a cop."

She took it in stride, the way she took everything. As he lay there she told him, "This is something we're gonna have to see about."

He left her then and went to his apartment. He grabbed his badge from where it was hidden behind the microwave beside his father's. Proven fact: burglars, thugs, smash and dashers, they'll tear a place apart, look in the sugar jar, in the coffee grounds, the ice cube tray, the toilet tank, but they always miss the tiny area behind the microwave. Probably worried they're going to somehow zap themselves.

He marched down to the club where Tucco and his left-hand man Cruez were in the back getting lap dances. He walked into the place and thought, I can shoot them both now and no one would care.

His lieutenant wouldn't mind. Even after twenty-six months, with all the evidence Crease had brought in, nobody wanted to make the case. They all wanted more. The mayor's office, the D.A., the narc squad, the vice squad. They wanted the connections, the inventories, the emperors and despots in South America who supplied the suppliers who supplied the bosses who ran the guys who ran guys like Tucco.

Crease would never get enough evidence for them to allow him to make the bust.

The girl dancing on top of Tucco had his belt in both hands, sliding them down. She stopped her grinding and got a spooked look, like she knew Crease was a cop. She wanted out of the room but Crease blocked the way.

The other one hanging on Cruez was too busy to turn around. The room was small, a lot of bad could happen there in very short order. Tucco's mouth was smeared with red lipstick, it made him look like he'd been chewing rabbits raw. He glared at Crease and said, "You think she's going to give me back my five hundred bucks?"

Crease said, "Listen, I'm a cop."

He flashed the badge, realizing later it was his old man's. It must've been an unconscious way to cause another problem. The more he thought about it, the more he realized he must've wanted to really get the ball rolling, give Tucco some clues, get his ass in gear. Tucco had a near-perfect memory. He'd instantly memorized the badge number and later gotten his tech boys to do a search on them, track them down. That's what led him to Hangtree.

If it had been his own badge, nothing would've come up. There were no files anymore. Everything about him was deleted. That must've been why he'd taken his father's instead.

Crease wondered why he did things like that.

Cruez climbed out from beneath the other stripper, who was so stoned that it took her a few seconds to realize he was gone. She was still making vaguely serpentine movements as he went for his gun. Crease took two steps forward and pressed his .38 under Cruez's blunt chin and said, "Not yet."

Tucco was smiling, always so sharp and way ahead of the game. "Put that thing away. Nothing's gonna happen.

Your friends on the force, they know what you've done for me?"

"They know."

"Your cell gonna be next to mine?"

"Probably not."

"You don't have your handcuffs out. You're not busting me. So you don't have enough for a case."

"I've got enough for fifty cases," Crease told him, "but they don't care. Nobody does. So no, I'm not busting you. I've got some unfinished business I've got to take care of first. I'll be gone a few days, no more than a week. When I get back, I'll look you up again, and we can settle whatever score we've got."

"Only score I see is the one you've been working."

"Maybe so."

"You're crazy, man," Tucco said. "I've never known one like you before."

"Be glad," Crease said and walked out.

In the back of the Bentley, he held onto Morena another minute. He pressed his forehead to hers and thought of everything he'd never told her. Maybe it would get through anyway. She didn't know he was married, didn't know about Stevie, but there was no time to get into it right now. He kissed her beneath her ear and she hummed at the back of her throat.

He didn't want to push Tucco too much at the moment. Cool as the guy was, and as much as he dug being shoved, Tucco might get a little wild about him and Morena making it in a two hundred thousand dollar car. Worried about the state of his interior if not his woman. She said, "You know what he was doing the whole ride up here? He was giggling."

Crease couldn't believe it and looked at her. "Really?"

She nodded. "He thought it was funny. He liked the way it all went down. You walking into the club that way, cowboy-style. He's dealt with hardasses and maniacs but never a man with your flair."

"Did you tell him you're pregnant?"

"Of course. He doesn't care. He was trying to get under my skin by saying he'd raise the baby after you were dead. Start him off dealing when he was seven or eight in the schoolyards. If it was a girl, get her out on the street early, vying for the pedo trade." Crease saw that Tucco had indeed gotten under her skin. Her eyes were hard as slate. "Like I wouldn't shoot him in the back of his head before I allowed that. I might just do it anyway."

Crease didn't have to worry about the baby. She'd do anything she had to in order to keep the kid out of the life. He eased against her once more, and when their mouths met they twisted harder with near-desperation in each other's arms, the kiss rearing into something else. Neither one of them broke off, neither of them breathing. Morena let out a low wildcat cry and Crease urged the thing on, the pain and the need, the wonder of the next minute.

He didn't know when it ended but when he dropped back against the seat she was two feet away, all the way over there.

"Why are you in this place?" she asked.

"I've got some old accounts to square, I think."

"You think?"

"I'm still trying to work things out."

"Which things?"

"It has to do with my father."

"Are you going to kill somebody?"

"Maybe not."

She shook her head a little sadly, like he was nowhere near in focus and never would be. "What are you going to do next?" Angling her chin at the window. "About him."

"We're gonna run around the block for another couple of days, and then we'll get past the rap and we'll see what happens."

She grabbed the sides of his face and looked him square in the eyes. "You can't beat him. You might be crazier than him, but he's faster. You can't win that way."

He didn't like hearing it out loud, in her voice, the truth that had been circling around in his head for days. Not only that he wasn't fast enough, but that he was nuts. He didn't mind walking the edge but he didn't want her seeing him there.

He was fast, he was so fast his hands moved without him, but Tucco was something else altogether. "You're probably right, but that doesn't change anything."

"What if I said I loved you and wanted you to be with me? That I had enough money to get away, start over?"

"I'd probably say I loved you and wanted to be with you too," he told her. He wasn't sure if either one of them really loved or could ever love the other one the way they should, but you did the best you could. "It'd give me more reason to fight, but it wouldn't affect the outcome much. That's what I'd probably say."

She released his face and poured herself another drink. "Go then, finish what you've got to finish. His patience is going to wear out soon, you don't have more than two more days."

"That's all I need," he said.

He'd have done all he could do by then, and would either have an answer or would give up. He expected to give up.

"Good," she said, "because I don't have much patience either. Oh, and don't be surprised if he kills somebody in this town first, just to ramp himself up. It might be somebody you know."

She opened the door and made him climb out over her.

Cruez was waiting in the street. Tucco was staring up the road. He glanced at Crease and said, "These llamas, they on farms?"

"Yeah."

"What if I told you all is forgiven? Really. You being a cop, it doesn't matter to me. I've got plenty on the payroll, and none of them helped me like you have. Never had better times with anybody else. There's no outlaw as good as a dirty cop. You're my right hand."

"What about me?" Cruez asked.

"You. How many times do I have to tell you? You, you're my *left* hand."

"Oh."

Crease knew there would be a lot of talk, but he hadn't expected it to be like this. Tucco was serious. It could all go back to the way it was. He could still work for the cops and still do what he did in the underground. Maybe quit the cops and just let himself go.

But Morena. And the baby.

Strange he should give up his wife and son to the life, but now, Tucco's mistress pregnant with his child—a kid he might never even hold—should somehow drive him from it.

What the hell did it mean?

"So?" Tucco said. "Open your mouth, tell me what you're thinking. Come on, you know what I say is true. I don't lie. You ready to pick up where we left off? Maybe start bringing in some chinks from Canada? Got that nice shipment of H coming up next week. Need you with me on that."

Tucco lied all the time, to everyone about everything. It was sort of funny to realize he thought he was honest, maybe even noble in his own way with the people who mattered to him. He had the straight face and dead gaze for everybody, and the lies poured out of him so easily that he often mistook them for sincerity.

"No," Crease told him.

"No? You sure about that, man?" He showed his teeth for an instant and then the smile, or the grimace, was gone. "You know what you're doing?"

"Yeah."

"I don't think you do. You're not yourself, and anybody who knows you, really knows you like I do, can see it. I think this place has got you all confused, it's screwing with your head. Coming back here, it was bad idea. All these trees, they'd drive anybody crazy. You're concrete and steel and asphalt. This clean air is killing you."

Maybe it was true. "Could be. How about you? How are you feeling?"

"It's making me sick too. So let's get the hell out of here and go home."

"In two days we'll see what we see," Crease said. "Until then, you go visit with the llamas, all right? Don't snuff any old ladies."

9

He tried Burke's hardware store first, but Sam Burke had already gone home for the day. A teenager putting away six-foot lengths of copper tubing told him the store would be closing up in ten minutes, it was already after six. Crease had let the time get away from him. Morena's scent was still on him and it was making him a little heady.

Crease asked the teen if Burke still lived out on Deerwood Road, and the kid told him he wasn't allowed to give out that kind of information. Crease got back in the 'Stang and got turned around twice before he remembered which direction Deerwood Road was in. Not everything from the past was that close to the surface.

He drove slowly into the hills and found the place pretty easily, as if it had always been intended that he wind up here. It didn't take much to get you believing in fate, thinking your life was wrapped around someone else's who you hardly even knew. For years the thread connecting you would go unnoticed, and then one day it started to tug from the other end and you got reeled in.

He parked the 'Stang out front and made his way up the wide walkway to the front door. He hadn't rung the bell yet when Burke appeared. Like he'd been perched in the window for hours, waiting for Crease to come along.

Sam Burke recognized Crease immediately. His bland expression upgraded fast. It twisted and crept across his face inch by inch, emotions fluctuating as they went along. Sadness, puzzlement, even disdain showed vividly before returning to the carefully engraved contours of apathy. It was a little spooky that the guy would be so on top of him like that.

They both stood there, waiting for something to promote the moment. The dead girl was there with them. Crease felt Teddy's presence growing stronger. Crease's father's ghost wafted between them all, the man wanting redemption or maybe just another bottle of booze in hell.

Burke finally moved aside and Crease stepped in.

The house smelled of furniture polish, floor wax, potpourri, fresh paint, and stale air. It was the aroma of somebody desperately trying to clean away events that could never be undone. Crease knew the windows would be spotless but painted shut. These were people who had closed themselves in with their pain in order to keep it alive. Mary's room would look no different now than it had seventeen years ago. Her belongings would've been touched and caressed many thousands of times, and every fingerprint washed away again. Burke probably napped in his daughter's bed, but the intense dreaming would be too much for him. The thread between them tightened up with every step Crease took.

Burke was perfectly groomed, almost prim. He wore a very short, well-kept beard. Every button on his shirt was buttoned—right to the collar, the cuffs. The fold in his trousers was sharp enough to slice paper.

Burke evoked constraint. Inhibition, pressure, duress. Someone who killed two hours every morning in the bathroom, spent the day at work assembling and arranging and coordinating, and then faded the rest of his night sitting on the center cushion of the couch. Not touching anything, not moving.

The living room had been decorated by a woman but you could tell it no longer contained her living touch. Everything had been arranged where it was a long time ago and never been moved. Mrs. Burke was dead or gone. The place was immaculate as a museum. Crease didn't want to make any quick moves for fear of breaking the solemn air around him.

There were no photos anywhere. He could understand why. You couldn't put out any of your parents or your in-laws or your dog without having a few of Mary too. And to put her photos in your line of sight would just be a reminder that you couldn't protect your own kid, that your faith in the police and your friends and your neighbors was totally misplaced.

"You look very much like your father," Burke said.

The thought of it shook Crease for an instant. It got his back up, the heat rushing along his spine. Then he realized Burke meant the way his father had looked before the downfall, back when he was still doing his duty.

At least it's what Crease hoped the man meant. "I'd like to talk to you, if I could."

"I can guess why you're here. All of us reach a particular crossroads, an apex, and eventually return to where we began. You've got a lot of gray in your hair. You're young to be having a mid-life crisis, but rest assured I know something about that." Burke spoke with a clipped, rushed speech. Very tight but very carefully enunciated. "Still, let me ask, don't you think it's simply a waste of time?"

Crease didn't know how to answer. Burke didn't wait for one though, and merely stepped past him into the living room.

"No," Crease said to the man's back.

"Of course it is. You're just having some other crisis of life or faith, and you thought coming back here would be the way to resolve everything. You're on a grand search, a journey of conscience. Perhaps you've left a wife home wherever it is you now come from. Yes? Perhaps children. An irritated employer, a job half done. You've dug yourself a hole, you're walking a wire in high wind, would you say? And all these things will be set right if only you can solve the case that smashed your father's career and ruined his life. Do you really expect to clean the blood off his hands at this late date?"

The guy was sharp all right. You couldn't sell him short just because he had his collar buttoned and his windows stuck shut.

"Not everything will be straightened out," Crease said. "But it's a loose end that I want to try to tie up."

He knew it was the wrong thing to say the moment it was out of his mouth.

Burke sat on the center cushion of the couch, crossed his legs and said, "Well, how touching. Is that how you see it? What happened to my daughter? The greed that spurred your father?" Maybe the man was inoculated, safe behind his austere wall. "I don't consider her murder a 'loose end' at all. Nothing dangling there, you see. Quite the opposite. Her death severed all ties. That's what death does. There's no point in dredging that all up. Digging up the dead. It's been so long. You not only look like your father, you act like him as well. Are you a police officer?"

Christ, Burke was on the ball. All this time in the house alone, thinking, it really exercised his gray matter. "Yes."

"Are you a good one?"

"Depends on who you ask."

"I'm asking you."

He hadn't thought about it for a while and wondered how Burke had managed to take control of the conversation the way he had. Crease had come here to ask questions, and in about two minutes flat Burke had him pinned beneath glass. Maybe he owed the man an answer, maybe not, but something about the house, and Burke's controlled energy and direct way of speaking, the way he peeled Crease apart with his gaze, made Crease feel like he should give it a shot.

"I'm effective because I spend my time down in the mud with the guys I'm trying to stop. I'm good at my job but that just means I'm rotten at everything else. You understand that?"

"It sounds as if you're striving for nobility."

"If that's what you heard then you're mistaken." And he was. Burke was burned up with a fever of his own.

"Perhaps," Burke said. "In any case, I think you should let the dead rest."

He was surprised to hear Burke speaking like that, no matter how far down the man had gone to get away from his pain. Crease felt his father's presence all the time, often very strongly, and thought Burke would never be able to let his murdered daughter go, not even if he wanted to. Especially when you lived in the same house where she'd lived, from where she'd been stolen.

"Is that what they're doing? Is Mary at rest?"

"Are you prodding me?"

"Would you want me to?"

Crease finally decided to sit in a chair opposite Burke. The cushion made a heavy rasping noise. No one had sat here for a hell of a long time. The sound took on a whole new meaning in the silent house.

"Mrs. Burke?" Crease asked.

"My wife no longer resides with me. To be truthful, I don't know where she is, it's been some years since I've seen her. Perhaps with her sister in Terrytown, Connecticut. Or . . . elsewhere. I have no idea."

It wasn't the kind of thing you could say you were sorry about, but there was no point. Crease looked around and couldn't help thinking about security. No burglar alarm. No lock on the front screen door. No deadbolt. A good second-story man could get up onto the roof, and the screens could easily be popped out of the window frames. Just like he used to do when climbing up to Reb's room.

He lit a cigarette—still only had the menthols on him, he had to get to a store soon—and was surprised when Burke didn't show any upset about smoking in the house.

Crease leaned forward and pulled a shining glass ashtray close to him.

He said, "Tell me what happened."

"What's the point?"

"Maybe there is none. But explain it to me anyway. Give me the details."

"Don't you already know them?"

All that Crease knew about Mary's kidnapping, and everything that followed, was mired in memories of his own shame and urge to run. He had to start over, disconnect from it, get it clear. "Not in the broader sense."

"How broad a sense do you want them?"

Crease sat back, took a deep drag, and said, "How about if you quit running me around the block and just tell me what happened the day Mary was taken?"

The voice got a rise out of Sam Burke, who raised his chin an extra inch like he was expecting to get jabbed. He folded his hands over his knee and focused himself, going way deep inside. Crease could see him diving.

"This isn't about my little girl. This is about you and your father. That's the only reason you're interested. For your own selfish reasons. "

"So what? Crease said. "Maybe I can get done what the others were never able to do."

"I don't see how."

"You don't have to see how."

"Your father killed her."

"I know that."

Sam Burke sat waiting for more. It was going to be a long wait. Crease had never apologized for his old man and wasn't about to start now. Saying you were sorry for somebody else, ten years dead, just wasn't going to get the job done.

Crease wondered if Burke would get some kind of a kick out of hearing how he went to the mill and ran around pointing his finger and going bang bang, pretending to be his father, imagining the girl right there in front of him. Probably not.

"You've got nothing to lose," Crease said.

"Don't I? Are you quite so sure of that? Because you shouldn't be, no, you truly shouldn't be, I would say. Every time I see her photo, every mention of her name, the name 'Mary', I lose myself. Can you understand that? Can you possibly know what I mean? I disappear, I cease to exist for an instant. I go someplace where my girl is still with me, where she is looking up into my eyes, and holding my hand, and my wife is not in Terrytown or elsewhere. I vanish off the earth. And then I come back, you see. There's the trouble. That I come back. And yes, she's still dead, and I am alone, and the things that once mattered most can matter no longer. So I say to you, I do have something to lose, and it will be very costly to me to lose any more of it."

So that's how it was for him. Crease got it now.

He'd been wrong. Burke didn't have nearly as much control over himself as he did over his environment. The man was ready to shake loose at any second. He didn't want to say anything more, but his mouth wouldn't stop working. You could tell it panicked him, but it had been so long since he'd spoken about Mary that he couldn't turn it off.

"You know what she enjoyed doing more than anything else? Playing hide-and-seek. It was more than a child's game, you see. This house is over one hundred and twenty years old. There are many nooks and niches in it, places for a little girl to hide herself away from the world. She would grab something from us—my watch, her mother's gloves or some kitchen utensil, and she would run. She would hide. A girl who likes to hide so much came out into the open and was stolen from our own yard. Yes, that's what happened. Appalling. She stepped into the open and was shot down by the sheriff whose duty it was to get her home safely again. Don't you find that ironic?"

"No," Crease said. "I find it tragic."

"You only say that because it is," Burke said. "I'm vanishing, you know. Inch by inch, I'll soon be gone."

Crease could see it happening. He thought, this guy, he doesn't have much longer to go. Maybe if Crease could get some answers, Burke would start seeing himself in the mirror again.

Burke's clipped, darting style of speech went on and on. "There isn't much to tell, really. It was the fifth of June, a warm day, a sunny day, but not especially hot. Mary didn't want to wear long sleeves, she hated long sleeves, and she and Vera—my wife, Vera—fought about that, but not much, really, and Mary usually won such battles anyway. She was just going to play in the back yard, alone, with some dolls and their accessories. Everything has accessories, the cars and the pools and the wardrobe for the dolls, an entire city set up in the yard. She was very popular, Mary was, she had many friends in the neighborhood, but that day she was alone."

"You were home?"

"Until noon or so. I went in to work late, being the owner does have some advantages. I spent the morning watching a film I wished to watch. A documentary on VHS, rented right next door to my hardware store, Bob's Video. It's not there anymore. Don't ask me which documentary it was, I don't recall. I remember a great deal about that day, but not the film I wanted to watch so badly that I spent the morning at home. Afterwards, Mary, Vera, and I had lunch together— chicken salad. I didn't say goodbye to her. She ran out the back door to play and I left through the front. Vera followed me down the driveway to get the mail from the box, and I drove off. An hour later, she phoned me at the store. Mary was gone."

Crease stubbed out his cigarette. "Had they made contact yet?"

"No. I rushed home and we searched the house . . . we thought perhaps she was playing hide-and-seek again, although Mary never did this when we spoke firmly with her and demanded she show herself. She would always come out then, smiling, happy to have fooled us for so long, and that was all right. It was always all right so long as she showed herself when we finally asked, you see? But she didn't come out that day. We searched the yard, we visited our neighbors, we called the police. I—"

Here it comes, Crease thought.

"—spoke with your father." Burke wasn't able to keep the hostility out of his voice, and the fever started up in Crease's chest, began to burn. "He told me he'd be right over. It took less than ten minutes. He was very powerfully built, your father, with an air of authority. He seemed very assertive, effective, despite the recent death of his wife. I'd always found him trustworthy, even though at that moment I smelled the alcohol on his breath. But I was a near-sniveling mess. Vera was already in shambles. We held onto each other and dragged ourselves around together like cripples. The phone rang again. It was a man. A voice I'd never heard before. He said he had Mary. He would return her for the sum of fifteen thousand dollars. He was specific in his instructions. No police."

"But my father was already there."

"Yes, you see, your father was already there. I couldn't even follow his demands because the sheriff was already there."

"What did the man on the phone say exactly?"

"He was brief. He wanted fifteen thousand dollars. He wanted me to bring it to the abandoned mill and leave it. No police involvement. Mary would be returned to us within twenty-four hours without harm."

"How easy was it for you to get your hands on that kind of money?"

"Very easy," Burke said. "We weren't especially well-to-do, but fifteen thousand dollars isn't an outrageous sum of money. We had sixty thousand in our savings. It seemed like such a ridiculous amount to ask for in exchange for the life of our daughter."

"Yes, it does."

Burke made as if to change position, maybe move over on the couch an inch, but then he resettled himself to the same position."The details, do they still need to be so broad, or are you familiar with what happened afterwards?"

"The dolls," Crease said. "Were any missing? Broken?"

"Only her teddy bear. It was her favorite, her sidekick as it were. Her best friend. The other dolls were toys that she *and* Teddy both played with, you see?"

"Snatched out of the yard. That points to someone she knew. You didn't recognize the man's voice, so it was probably a two-person team. Children are more likely to be lured away by women. They feel safer."

"I don't recall anyone telling me that before. In any case, everyone knew her. She was friendly like that. We all were. My wife and I, back when we were together. This was a nice town, or so we all thought. Sarah didn't agree, but she was growing more fond of Hangtree as time went on."

"Sarah?" Crease asked.

Burke's head cocked, like it was a name he hadn't heard in so long that he didn't recognize it despite just having said it. "Yes, Sarah, my older sister. Older by nearly four years. Mary's aunt. She was living with us at the time. Recuperating. She'd suffered through a broken relationship."

"Was she home that day?"

"No. No, she wasn't. She'd gone to spend the day in the park. To read and relax." Burke was clearly speaking by rote, repeating what his sister had told him, word for word.

"Can I speak with her?"

"No, I'm afraid not. It wouldn't be worth your time, you see. She's . . . unresponsive."

Crease waited for Burke to tell him more, but the man didn't continue. His energetic burst of speech had come to a standstill. The man's eyes were now glazed. He was going even deeper. Crease said, "I don't understand."

"My sister has had a great deal of upset in her life. She loved Mary so much, almost like she was her own daughter, really. When we lost her, she . . . well, she collapsed. She's never recovered, I'm told."

"Where can I find her?"

Burke's face tightened, his features folding in on themselves. "I don't want you visiting and bothering her."

"Who was the man from the broken relationship? What other upset did she have?"

"I don't want you to see her and I don't wish to discuss this any longer. I think it's time for you to leave."

Crease waited. He watched Burke wrestling with himself, thinking of his dead daughter, his absent wife, all of the pain throbbing under his face, pulsing, like it would shatter his flesh and come flying through the shards at any second.

"What other upset?" Crease asked.

"As I said, a broken love affair. We've all had them. Are you going to tell me you haven't?"

"No."

"Then, it's settled," Burke said.

"What's settled?"

"This discussion. It's over. I hope you understand, surely you do, but quite simply I don't wish to speak with you any longer. There's nothing you can do for me. Nothing that can be done for Mary. Or your father. He's dead and good riddance to him. To think I stood in awe of him once, in my own home. How pitiful, how foolish." He reached over and drew the now dirty ashtray closer to him, pulled it into his lap like it was a child. "You've accomplished absolutely nothing. Now, leave. Please leave."

Crease stood and walked out the door.

He thought, Okay, that was easy.

10

He was in a downtown bar parking lot, at a payphone trying to call Joan, when he heard them walk up around him. They coughed and kinda muttered, sniffing loudly, scuffling their feet. A sure sign of hesitation.

Crease sighed and put the phone back in its cradle and turned to meet them.

There was Jimmy Devlin and three other guys who might as well have been Jimmy. All of them cut from the same colorless cloth, ex-jocks who'd gone to flab but still had a lot of brawn. Mooks who'd discovered too late that running touchdowns might get them laid by a cheerleader but it wasn't going to get them anywhere far in the world.

The disappointment scrawled in their faces was offset by a perpetual confusion, like they still didn't understand where their lives had taken the left turn. Forty years down the line, they'd still be wearing that expression in their coffins.

These guys, Crease imagined them taking out their old trophies, hissing hot breath against them, and wiping them down with a greater gentleness than they'd ever shown their wives or kids. He had nothing but disdain for these kinds of mooks because in an adjacent universe he was one of them.

He still had Jimmy's knife sheathed on his belt. He drew it and held it out to him, handle-first. "Hey, you want this back? It's okay, I've got another one now."

Jimmy—all four Jimmys—stared at Crease like they didn't know what to make of him. They had no idea how dangerous this was yet, how fast things could go nuclear. Funny how many guys walk around looking mean, flexing what muscle they have left, doing their best to appear brutal, but then act all baffled when somebody takes them seriously.

He saw the bulge of a .32 under one of their jackets. It wasn't in a holster, just stuck in the guy's tight inside pocket like it wasn't any big deal. If he had to draw it in a hurry, he'd be dead before he got his hand on it.

The others weren't carrying. They had no leader. Each one of them was waiting for the other to make the first move.

Jimmy Devlin didn't move to take his knife, so Crease put it back on his belt. He thought about playing around with the butterfly blade for a minute, see what kind of impression it made on these idiots, the speed he could work it, but he didn't want to go to the trouble. It would be easier and more practical to nip this as quick as possible.

Jimmy Devlin's nose was taped up, but Crease knew he hadn't broken it. Jimmy actually took a step backward, trying to center himself, one fist covering his solar plexus to ward off another punch there.

The other Jimmys, now a step out in front, didn't know which way to move, forward or back. They shuffled around some more.

Maybe Crease hadn't come back to town because of his father. Maybe the girl's murder didn't mean as much to him as it should have. Maybe it was just for this kind of scene right here that he'd bolted north. Because no matter how old you got, how much you saw or did, how many children you had or medals you stowed, the adolescent pain clung to your back like a clawed animal.

Jimmy pointed a finger at Crease and said, "You! You screwing my girl?"

"You want me to?" Crease asked.

"No! What kind of sick question is that?"

Sometimes they were too dumb to even toy with. "You boys sure you want to do this?"

"Do what?" one of the others said, and he cracked his knuckles. The rest chuckled and bared their teeth in befuddled, bitter smiles, trying to ramp themselves up.

The taped nose caused Jimmy Devlin's voice to go high and nasal. He sounded like his testicles hadn't descended yet. "Where'd you come from, huh? Why are you here? I want to know why you're here."

"I wish I could answer that, I really do," Crease told him. "But the truth is, I'm not certain myself. Let's just say I needed to see Hangtree again. And there's some stuff about my old man. And kidnappers. And a serious drug dealer and a bent sheriff. And a dead six-year-old girl. And money."

"What money?" one of the other Jimmys asked, his eyes wide.

The setting sun dropped heavily from the sky, the silhouettes of distant stands of pine and maple raised against its face. Night swarmed in around them, the stars appearing in great moving washes like a black ocean stirring as a storm approached. Wind swept across the street and blew bronze leaves with slashes of fiery ember along the walks. Inside the bar things were starting to crank, the dull thrum of music and belligerent laughter rising and falling in swells. Front porch wind chimes tinkled and tolled up and down the roads, all across the neighborhood. He didn't hear any children laughing. He seemed to want to hear children laughing. He was getting maudlin again.

Jimmy Devlin said, "You aren't from here, are you?"

"I could read you the license plate of your orange '84 Camaro, if you want. But you probably don't remember it, do you, Jimmy?"

"Christ, you do know me."

"I know you."

"I want your name. Tell me your name."

"No," Crease said.

There was always a problem with talking too much, even if you only did it to squeeze a little entertainment out of the situation for yourself. You got to chattering and pretty soon the others started believing you weren't going to do anything more. You were all talk. It gave them time to quell their nerves and pump themselves up again. Crease knew he should shut up, but he couldn't help himself. Talking to Jimmy was scratching a few places deep inside him that he hadn't fully realized he still had.

He could see these four on the streets of New York, swaggering downtown in the East Village. Looking for a place to get a brew and the first spot they hit is a gay bar. They walk in and see two guys holding hands and suddenly they need to start bashing in order to prove to each other they didn't want to take bubble baths together. They'd get half an insult out before they got their asses kicked.

Crease sighed again.

Another Jimmy said, "Answer the man. The man wants an answer. You should give him one. You're being rude."

"What's that?"

"You're being very disagreeable!"

It got Crease grinning. He thought, That's the worst the guy can say? That I'm *disagreeable*?

Another Jimmy said, "Yeah, who do you think you are? You coming around here causing all kinds of trouble. Irritating our friend. Screwing around with his girl. Asking sick questions. We don't like people who ask sick questions around here."

Jimmy with the .32 said, "Don't make us do something we don't want to do."

"Like what?" Crease asked.

"Like what we don't want to do."

"Yeah, but what is it you don't you want to do?"

"We don't want to do something you might make us do!"

"What am I making you do?"

"Just get in your car and get out of here. Or else you might make us—"

Taking a step forward and getting back in line with the others Jimmy Devlin said, "Just stay away from Rebecca. She's my girl."

"You sure about that?"

"You don't know her, you don't know who you're dealing with. You got no idea what she's all about." He let out that laugh again, the one from the old days. "You should've listened to me when I was talking to you the other night. She'll spit you out. I love her. You can't handle her."

Crease heard that laugh and everything that went along with it, the sound of the Camaro's engine kicking into fourth gear. The tires squealing down Main Street, the smash of the beer bottle. His old man saying, "Take cover."

The four Jimmys moved up another step, the two on the ends easing out in a wide spread, cutting off any exit. All of them dropping their shoulders, shifting their weight. They were on the front line. Coach had them by the birdcage. They probably saw bleachers around them all the time, girls waving in the stands. Talent scouts taking notes.

They were stupid and they would be easy, but the chances were high that at least one of them would get hurt badly. Or somebody would get a lucky punch in. Crease couldn't afford to be off his game when it came to the final drop with Tucco. He didn't need any more trouble right now. Not when the real thing would be coming along soon enough.

Crease said to Jimmy Devlin, "Let me get this straight, okay?"

"Okay," Jimmy Devlin said, being very *agreeable*.

"You gave Reb four hundred bucks for bills, then two weeks later she tells you that you stink, sends you to the shower, steals two bottles of Jack and a hundred and eighty bucks out of your wallet." Crease had a good memory too. It threw guys off, hearing their own stories word for word coming back at them. "Then she lures you to the diner fifteen miles out of town, steals the plastic jug at the gas station, makes you an accomplice after the fact, then tries to ride off with a trucker. You slap her around some and she runs inside, meets me, has me work you over even while she's telling you to work me over. All this, and she's still your girl, you want her back. You love her. That right?"

The other three Jimmys looked at the fourth, waiting to hear his answer. Nobody could put the pressure on you like your best friends. Especially when they thought you were losing your manhood to a chick who treated you like trash.

Crease lit a cigarette and leaned back against the phone, letting their eyes do all the work for him.

Jimmy Devlin said, "This isn't about her right now, it's about you jumping me the other night. Doctor's bill was eighty bucks and he couldn't do anything for me but tape my face up. I'm pissing blood from those cheap shots you gave me."

Enough of the tension had dispersed from the situation. Crease walked up close. The Jimmys had a tough time holding their ground. They didn't move their feet but they reared their chins back. Jimmy with the .32 stuck his chest out, like the pistol would protect him somehow even in his pocket.

Crease said, "She's not worth the aggravation. You're a bigger man than that, Jimmy Devlin. Go on out with your boys tonight and they'll help you hook up with a real woman, one who won't treat you as poorly as Reb has. You deserve much better. Give your heart away more carefully, to someone who will value it."

He'd been forced to say much more important things with a straight face before, but it had never been quite so tough. He stuck the cigarette between his teeth and champed on it.

Another Jimmy said, "I never liked her much, to tell the truth. She always seemed to have an agenda, that one."

Another Jimmy said, "We're only thinking of you, man. You need somebody new. Wife material, like my Betty. She's got friends, I think we could probably fix you up with somebody nice, if you want."

Jimmy with the .32 said, "Remember Lydia Miller? You always liked her. She's getting divorced and only has one kid. A four-year-old. They're not much trouble at that age. They usually sleep through the night."

Jimmy Devlin said, "Lydia's getting divorced? I didn't know that."

"I told you."

"You never told me."

"I told you over at Bammer's house a couple of weeks ago, but you were stewing over Reb. It happened fast, Lydia and Stan breaking up. Stan had a gambling problem, was always at the Indian Reservation."

"I saw him there a couple times."

"He took a second mortgage out without even telling her and eventually lost his job. Pretended to go to work every day and would go to the strip clubs for their brunch buffet."

"I didn't know that."

"Lydia was in the dark until one day she answers the door and it's the bank, guy serving her papers. She packed up the kid and her belongings on the spot and went home to her parents. They got a nice basement apartment."

Another Jimmy said, "She's got to look after her kid's welfare. I bet a responsible guy would impress her—"

The music and laughter inside throbbed out an invitation. The parking lot lights snapped on, humming and burning. Beyond, the dark sky frothed over the final rays of the sun.

Crease finished up his cigarette, flicked the butt off into the dark, turned back to the phone and started dialing a number, thinking that the Greenwich Village boys definitely would've had a frickin' field day.

11

Tucco's tech whiz kids weren't really in the loop so Crease figured it was safe enough to give them a whirl. The word that Crease was a cop probably hadn't filtered down yet, even though they're the ones who would've looked up his father's badge number. They had the info and didn't have the info, that's what the tech boys were so good for.

He got a whiz kid and gave him Sarah Burke's name and all the relevant information he had on hand, which wasn't much. It didn't have to be. Within two minutes the kid spit back the name of a state-run assisted living group home where she'd been shuffled off to after banging around mental hospitals for the better part of a decade. The kid MapQuested the address and gave Crease the directions. Turned out to be just over the New Hampshire state line in a town called Langdaff.

It would be after ten by the time he got there and he wasn't sure what the rules of the place would be. Did you have to call ahead and make an appointment? Could you walk up off the street? Did you have to be family to visit? He decided to give it a go anyway, and if need be, he'd find a cheap spot to stay overnight and try again in the morning.

The Jimmys were still dialoguing. Crease got in the 'Stang, gassed up around the block, drove out to the interstate and headed to New Hampshire.

The directions were perfect and went right down to the tenth of a mile when the next turn was coming up. He made it in no time, listening to an Oldies station, his mind a flat, empty lowland periodically broken by someone running by in the distance.

The group home was a converted Victorian house that on the open market would bring in one point two, one point three mil. A sign on the front lawn said it was the Sinclair Mayridge Home for the Needful. It sounded like a methadone clinic in Harlem.

Crease parked at the curb and stepped up. Several people sat on the porch conversing lazily. One guy was reading a paper, two women convened in the corner crocheting and discussing what sounded like a romance novel. A teenage boy leaned against the railing where he typed on a laptop, and a teenage girl sidled at his shoulder watching him. Nobody looked particularly needful. They all looked well-rested and happy as hell.

Crease climbed the stairs but wasn't sure what the etiquette was. If you were supposed to knock or if you just walked right in. He looked around wondering if anybody would make eye contact and give him a hint, but nobody seemed to notice him. He turned the knob and wandered inside.

More blithe folks sat in a living room watching television, pleasantly chatting. If anybody was in charge, he couldn't tell who it might be. He lit a cigarette and two middle-aged ladies playing cards told him in unison, "No smoking here."

He ground the butt out against his heel and said, "Sarah Burke?"

"Upstairs. Room twelve."

He took the stairs two at a time, feeling like a thief in the night. Strange it should be that way since nobody cared he was here. Still, he could just imagine someone leaping out of a chair and pointing at him, screaming hideously, falling into convulsions. Somebody might slip a dirty pair of panties in his pocket and send him up the river for a nickel.

Door ten was painted yellow. Eleven was green. Twelve orange. Flowers and bunnies and other cuddly creatures had been carefully depicted on each of them. Rainbows arced across the walls of the hallway, multicolored groups of children danced harmoniously across blue globes. Crease thought he could very easily bug out in a place like this.

Someone had snuck Jesus way up top, almost on the ceiling, smiling down upon the puppies and tulips. One of the needy could call a lawyer and start yelling about the separation of church and state, maybe walk out of this place with a laundry bag full of money.

He knocked on the door of room twelve. No sound from inside, and he got no sense of movement. He knocked again. He imagined the woman in there staring at the door, wishing lethal thoughts through the wood, into his head. Willing murder, demanding death, spilling blood from afar.

You could get yourself pretty jazzed in front of a closed door in a state-run facility.

He swung it open and walked in.

A forty-watt bulb burned through a smoke-stained, dust-covered lampshade, giving the room a sickly yellow pallor.

Sarah Burke was seated in a ladder-back wooden chair in the far corner, huddled inside a ratty cotton nightgown. Her slippered feet didn't quite touch the floor. It was a crazy place to be, sitting over there far away from the rest of the furniture, the windows, the closet, everything. She was drawn up into herself—her body twined against and within itself—staring out at everything else like she found it all so peculiar.

A bony, ragged face, all you really saw were her eyes.

He'd dealt with a lot of bad dudes in his time, but only a couple of them had ever given him the willies on sight. She did it to him. Plucked a nerve deep inside that you never wanted touched. Some people, you just looked at them and knew the seriously bad juju was at work. It was all over her.

Her white hair stuck out in clumps and tufts. This was a witch, a queen gone bad in the deep forest who plotted your death while she fed you gingerbread cookies. Stevie's kiddie books were filled with creepy broads like this. She was so thin that he found it hard to believe her bones didn't break just carrying out the most casual acts. Just walking across the room would cause her kneecaps to burst through her skin.

He remembered he'd thought something similar about her brother, Sam Burke. Sitting there in his living room with his anguish pulsing under his face, pulsing, like it would come crashing through his flesh at any second.

She was needful all right. What she needed you couldn't give her. If you could give it to her then you'd be as wracked across the rocks as she was.

Crease said, "I'd like to talk to you."

The woman turned her lifeless eyes on him. She stared hard, harder than most people were able to do no matter the reason. You couldn't get angry enough to glower that way. You couldn't be thoughtful enough. It was something that happened when you went so deep in the well that you couldn't climb back out again.

Yeah, the lady had taken a fall and dug in when she hit the ground. He cocked his head and studied her another minute.

We're going home, Teddy.

The fever scrambled over him again. The sweat flowed down his neck and back, his scalp prickled. Soon his hair was dripping and his face was wet, the taste of salt flowing into his mouth. If nothing else, it perked her up. Her tiny body began to churn in the chair. He did the math. Burke had said she was older than him by four years. That made her no more than maybe fifty on the outside.

She grinned at him and Crease grinned back. She drew her chin back and her wrinkled lips dropped back into place. She said, "You my new neighbor? You number thirteen?"

"No."

"They always say no. All the thirteens say no."

"I guess they were lying then. I'm not."

"What do you want from me? I don't have anything for you." She started slowly nodding, certain of something. "You're sweating. It's not hot in here. Why are you sweating like that?" Her feet began to swing, the bottom of the slippers slapping her heels with each pass. "None of the other thirteens sweated."

"I want to talk about Mary."

The name got to her.

Sarah Burke was gone but not as gone as she wanted everyone to think. Her eyes cleared and she tilted her chin at him. Her brow knotted, the bottom lip quivered and drooped. He saw a pink flash of jutting tongue. Her hands gripped the arms of the chair, and the tendons stood out in her forearms as clear as polished marble.

"Who are you?" she asked.

"Tell me what happened, Sarah," he said.

"No."

He walked to the window nearest her. The shade was drawn. He tugged on it and the shade inched up over the glass. A ray of moonlight stabbed into the room and she flailed in her chair.

"Don't do that, thirteen," she told him. "My eyes, I've got a condition."

"I bet I know what it is. Tell me what happened to Mary."

"I could yell, you know. I could scream."

"You've been screaming for seventeen years. How about if you just talk to me instead?"

The condition of her eyes grew worse as the memories began to burn through her mind. He saw it happening, one small flame igniting a patch of dry woodland. The fire spreading, leaping across treetops, spanning all the hidden acres marked off with barb wire. It was alive and inescapable.

The blaze ran rampant as if on a mission. Sarah Burke sat gaping and wide-eyed with only purified, burning sparks of remembrance left behind in her head.

It made her slump even further down in the chair. Her feet were now swinging so fast that both slippers had launched across the room. He tried to enforce his will over her, make her spit out the truth. She seemed to be slowing down, waking up. Crease wondered why she'd outlasted all the thirteens next door.

He walked over and sat on her bed. It was a basic psychological ploy. You made yourself at home, showed them that you were there to stay, that what was theirs was now yours. He shifted the pillows behind him and lit a cigarette.

Sarah Burke stared at him with a kind of grudging respect.

Surrendering she said, "Where do you want me to start?"

"You know where."

"I suppose I do."

He waited, and time drifted quaintly in the house. The screen door slammed and the other needy occupants took advantage of the state of New Hampshire's and Sinclair Mayridge's good graces and settled in for the night. Doors opened and shut around the home. Toilets flushed, a shower went on.

Finally he had to prod her by saying, "With the upset."

"I've had a few. Haven't you?"

"Yes. Talk about the first one that counted."

She let out a cackle. It went on and on as the bones in her small body grated against one another. He could vividly picture her throwing back her head and letting that noise go on for another half minute before leaping out of the chair and diving through the window. Crease got ready to tackle her if need be.

But instead the laughter ended as abruptly as if she'd been strangled. "Who are you?"

"Tell me about the broken love affair."

"I've had a few of those too."

"No," Crease said. "I don't think you have."

"You're right, I'm too ugly. Hardly any man would ever have me."

"Just tell about the one who mattered. The one that meant everything to you."

What was inside her began to move closer to the surface. He could almost see it there in the black depths, rising, fighting to break free.

"What was his name, Sarah?"

That's all it took. The legs stopped swinging. She untwisted a little, and groaned from somewhere in the center of her chest as if awakening from a long sleep. The unfolding of her body became the unfurling of her past.

She drew her fingers through her hair and brushed it back across her head, and the witchy lady became just another battered woman who looked twenty years older than she was. He had arrested her many times. Under Tucco's tutelage he had created many variations of her.

She said, "Daniel. Daniel Purvis. He was a gambler."

"Ah."

"He couldn't help himself. It was a sickness. It had nothing to do with money, but with the excitement, the rush it gave him. He'd ride his truck on empty to see how much farther it would go. He'd pass a gas station and get a wild thrill that he'd made it that far, and then he'd still keep going, and pass another, and another. He always ended up stuck on the side of the road. Always. You ever meet anybody like that?"

Everybody had, whether they knew it or not. "Yes."

"Daniel was the only one who ever showed any interest. I was never pretty. Men made me feel ashamed. But not Daniel. He held me. He talked to me. He made me happy. Whispered my name. Can you understand that?"

"Yes."

She had a few psychological ploys of her own. Throwing it back in Crease's lap, so he sympathized. Maybe she'd picked it up off her psychiatrists on the mental wards.

"My family didn't approve. They tried to wedge themselves between us. My brother hated Daniel. He kept telling me to wait for someone better, a man who would truly love me. He always stressed the *truth* of love, but never understood what that meant. The truth of love is that you accept what's wrong and ugly and stupid and tainted in your lover. Sam is a very foolish and naive man. Ultimately, that's the reason why Vera left him." She glanced over at Crease and said, "May I have a cigarette?"

He got off the bed and offered her the pack. She stared at it in disgust. "Are those menthol?"

"All the store had left."

"Take it away."

He reseated himself and waited for her to get back into the rhythm of telling her story. It only took a minute.

"But Daniel couldn't control himself. His gambling grew worse. He couldn't stay away from the casinos. He played poker with strangers. No matter how much he had, he always owed more. He got into trouble. He was beaten once, not so badly. Then he was beaten again, much worse." She started speaking in speedy, clipped sentences devoid of any emotion, exactly as her brother had done. "Men were going to kill him. I begged my parents for money and they refused. Yes, they refused me. I knew my brother would deny me as well. Daniel couldn't hold off those brutes any longer. So you know what they did? I'll tell you. They tied him to the bumper of his pickup truck and drove it into a cement retaining wall. They crushed his right leg. The doctors had to amputate. He told the police nothing. I cared for him as best I could after that, while he recuperated, playing cards on his hospital bed. But all that mattered was money then. Every knock on the door, every phone call. Everything had become about money, no longer merely the thrill. There was nothing else."

He didn't want to tell her that it was that way for most people all of the time, so he just nodded.

"And still he owed the men who had taken his leg. That wasn't payment. I thought it would be enough payment in itself, the taking of his leg, but no, I was wrong. It didn't count, you see? It didn't cover a dime of debt, his blood and muscle and bone. His becoming a cripple. He still owed."

That was standard too. You didn't let the guy off after you broke his arm, cut off his thumb, or burned his house down. That was just the interest, you still had to pay the principal.

"What was his game at the casino? Craps?"

"Blackjack and roulette."

Daniel Purvis really was a sucker.

"So let me guess," Crease said. "He was in a fifteen thousand dollar hole."

"Ten."

That surprised Crease. Ten g's usually wasn't enough to get the legbreakers out breaking legs. Then again, in Vermont, who knew. It was a spooky place compared to New York.

It also proved that Sarah Burke wasn't just trying to get the beau out of debt. She'd gotten greedy along the way. Another five grand to give them a head start someplace else, and her brother paying for it. Or maybe it was a show of love to Purvis, giving him the extra five g's as a gift. An extra pop to the addict, fill him full of bliss.

The rest of the house was silent now. Moonlight slashed into the room through the two inches of window pane Crease had uncovered when pulling up the shade. The slice of silver collapsed across the feeble, diseased yellow of the lamp. Shadows clung to the woman like cobwebs.

They sat there like that for a while, facing each other with their separate burdens which had somehow overlapped. Crease knew she was working up to it, to the act that had put her here as an escape from herself.

The mattress was soft and smelled faintly of some kind of citrus detergent, reminding him of Reb's bed.

"It was Daniel's idea," Sarah Burke said. "And of course I didn't argue. I didn't mind, not really. I hated my brother too much by then. I didn't put up any kind of resistance. The suggestion made sense, and even if it hadn't, I wouldn't have cared. I'd have done anything for him. That's the truth of love." She shifted in her seat and her bones rubbed against each other inside her like dry kindling. Crease had seen crack addicts under piles of garbage who looked healthier. He wondered how much longer she could possibly live.

"How did it go down?"

"As easy as warm apple pie. I gathered Mary up in my arms, and Daniel called my brother Sam and demanded the ransom. Fifteen thousand dollars. I knew he had it on hand, in the bank if not in his store safe. I never thought he would call the police and endanger her that way. I thought he would follow our simple set of rules. In fact, at the time, I believed he'd know right off that it was me, and finally realize how much Daniel meant to me. You see, I thought he would give me the money out of understanding and kindness. That he would finally acknowledge how much I loved Daniel. That he would give it to us as a favor. A wedding gift. Mary hardly entered the matter at all. I cared deeply for her, or thought I did, up until that point, you see?"

Crease didn't. He couldn't. He had never loved anyone the way Sarah Burke had loved the one-legged gambler Purvis. Maybe his father. He'd been willing to give up a lot of his life to his father, but only because he hadn't known what else he could possibly do.

"And then?" he urged.

Sarah began to coil again. Her fingers tightened on the arms of the chair, the tiny legs started swinging once more. They were getting down to it now, to the real venom. He knew that in a very real way he was finishing her off.

"And then?" he repeated.

"And then came the part you're most ʻeager to hear about, thirteen," she said. "Daniel and I wanted to trade her back for the money up at the old sawmill. It was the perfect setting, no one could possibly sneak up on us there. They were morons to try. My tightwad brother cared more for his money than his daughter, and far more than me. He called the sheriff. He sent that drunk, stumbling thief of a sheriff after us and we were all doomed after that. All of us."

Crease said, "It was your fault it went down the way it did. Purvis didn't call your brother soon enough after the snatch. They didn't know it was a snatch at first. They thought she might've just wandered away. That's why Sam called the sheriff. He was there when Purvis finally phoned. Your brother couldn't play it any other way, he had to work with the police. You botched it from the go."

Another pregnant pause in the room of the needy. Maybe he should check in next door for a while, catch up on his cool, be the thirteen. Nobody even came around to make sure the loonies were tucked into bed.

Sarah Burke's mouth opened and her tongue slid out like a leech. She had spent seventeen years trying to soothe her guilt with the idea that her crime of passion had made it worthwhile. There was enough blame to go around. The bent sheriff, her spiteful brother. She didn't like hearing that Purvis had screwed the pooch from the start. Six-year-old Mary Burke had never stood a chance.

"How do you know so much?" she asked.

"A Ouija board told me. You and Purvis took Mary to the mill together?"

"Yes, we were there, the three of us. We thought—I thought—that my brother would arrive and drop off the money and I would push Mary out to him. He would look in my face and see my love for Daniel and he would leave the ransom behind and go home. I would leave with Daniel and never see either of them again. That's why I kept telling Mary that I loved her and she should always hold in her heart, forever and ever, that Aunt Sarah loved her. I told her that even when she was much older she could always rely on it, you see? That Aunt Sarah was thinking of her, that she would always love her Mary."

Crease reached down and grabbed the side of the box spring, and his grip tightened until the material began to rip and the springs inside squealed. Sarah looked at him and said, "Are you sick?"

"Yes, I'm sick."

"Me too, thirteen. I have some pills here. Would you like some?"

"No."

"Good, they're poison. For me anyway. They're killing me. I'm allergic but they keep giving them to me and I keep taking them. It will make things easier in the end for everyone."

He shut his eyes and released the mattress, took a few deep breaths until the fever began to pass. "You were waiting at the mill. You saw the sheriff pull up."

"Of course. He parked over the ridge but he was heavy-footed. He couldn't hear himself, how loud he was."

No, Crease thought, because the first thing that goes when you're drunk is the hearing.

"What did you and Purvis do then?"

"We left," she said.

"What?"

Her gaze locked with Crease's and she nodded. "That's right, I pushed Mary forward and told her to go see the nice policeman. Daniel said he spotted someone else in the woods, and we left. There are logger trails criss-crossing the entire hill. We drove away on one of them."

"Without the money? You couldn't have walked away from it that easily."

"But we did," Sarah Burke said. "I didn't want my niece to be hurt, and I couldn't afford to lose Daniel, not under any circumstances. As I said, this wasn't a kidnapping. I didn't want ransom. I wanted a gift. A gift from my brother. When I realized I was to be denied, we left."

"Where did you set her free in the mill? The far side? The north side?"

"Yes, that's right."

Way on the opposite end of the factory. His father should've seen a little girl walking up on him, at that point. But he was there for at least five hours before he noticed she was there, and when he did, he shot her.

Crease tried to see it from different angles. Maybe Mary fell asleep and only awoke at sunset, when Edwards started his move on the mill. But no, it made no sense. Could she have tried to follow after Sarah and Purvis after they left? Wandered around in the woods, lost for hours, before she found herself back at the mill? Just in time to snuff it. Too big a coincidence. It didn't really play.

He eyed Sarah Burke. She wasn't lying.

"Daniel drove me into town. He let me off in front of my brother's store, and then he just kept driving. I never saw him again. Perhaps he was only using me to get money. Or to have someone to care for him, at least for a while. Maybe he had grown tired of me. I realized that was possible from the start. Perhaps he did it to protect me from the men who would soon be coming for him. But it—"

"It didn't matter," Crease said. "You didn't care."

"I didn't care, it didn't matter. Nothing did. Surely you see that."

He shook his head, kind of sadly, the way he did when he saw somebody about to do something stupid during a deal. Some idiot reaching for a gun, Tucco moving, Crease raising his .38, shaking his head.

"Not even the consequences," Sarah Burke said. "I understood what they would be. Even if we'd gotten the money and run away together, sooner or later he would've abandoned me. I'd have nowhere to go but home again to my brother's house. And then I'd go to jail."

"The police never questioned you?"

"Of course they did," she told him, "but Sam covered for me. You see, he knows I did it. He's always known, although he can't admit it to himself. That's why Vera left him. That's why he's so mincing and clean and proper. He can't relax. He can't let go. If he does, even for an instant, in any way, he'll vanish. That's what he says."

"Yes."

"That's what he's most afraid of—disappearing, the same way Mary did. The truth would destroy him. It may still." She let out a rictus smile that was no lip and all teeth. "As I've vanished. I suppose in my heart I always knew I'd wind up here or a place like it. There's no bars on the windows but I'm trapped. I dwindle. Where can I go? Where could I ever possibly go? I live in expectation. Every morning, every night, I fully expect him to walk through that door and kill me. I dream of it. I hope for it, you see. He thinks vanishing is a torture. For me, it would be a blessing. A godsend. Is that why you're here, thirteen? Did God send you after me?"

"No."

"Are you sure you won't share my poisonous pills?" she asked.

"No," he said, and started for the door, "you keep them all."

12

The rearview drew his eyes. The sense that someone was following him, or worse, hiding in the back seat, was overwhelming. Was it his old man, sitting there with a pint in his hand, vomit crusted on his shirt front? His father sobbing, wishing he had another chance to do things right, or maybe just to steal a little more. Crease couldn't tell.

Over the miles, the presence became much stronger. Maybe Mary, trying to tell him what a waste it had all been? He knew who'd killed her. He knew why it had happened. All that was left was finding the cash, and a dead girl wouldn't care about that.

Teddy on her lap, her small hands petting the bear, hugging it tight. What he'd done so far, what was the point of any of it?

Maybe it was Mimi's lost husband, longshoreman Lenny back there, who took off after the fourth or fifth kid, urging

Crease to just cut loose and keep running. Skip out while he still could.

Man, when you didn't have your cool left you really had nothing at all.

Halfway to Hangtree, the window down and the breeze coursing through the car, rushing against him even as his forehead burned and the windshield fogged, he felt a wistful ache. It took him a minute to recognize the emotion for what it was. He wanted to check on Joan and Stevie.

He hit a cheap motel along the highway, paid for the night, showered, settled in, and reached for the phone. It was almost midnight. Joan would be sleeping but she wouldn't be angry if he woke her. He wondered if there was anything he could do to make her furious. And if so—if he had found whatever it was in time—if it would've somehow saved their marriage.

He called Joan. He wanted to hear her voice. Even if he didn't feel like saying much, she'd understand and do all the talking, trying to soothe him about things she didn't understand. When you got down to it, that's probably why his son hated him so much. Not for what Crease had done to Stevie, but what he'd done to the boy's mother. The kid had real pride and felt as great a sense of responsibility to protect her as Crease had felt about his father.

Instead, Mimi answered. "Hello, who's that?"

"Mimi, what are you doing there?"

"Your back screen door has slipped out of the track. I tried to get it back in but it won't go, it's bent. You'll have to fix that. I don't want Freddy getting out. Your side gate doesn't close either, the little thing, what do you call it, the latch, you have to jiggle it so it'll lock, except it doesn't work."

Crease tried to remember if Freddy was the kid with the beady eyes, or if it was the dog. He said, "But why are you there?"

"I can't visit my sister?"

"You never visit your sister."

"I could if I wanted to, though. Anyway, my oven broke. I'm afraid of a gas leak, so I packed the kids in the car and brought them over here."

He pictured her house. "Mimi, you've got an electric stove."

"What?"

"You have an electric stove, didn't you realize that?"

"How do you know? All of a sudden you're a mister fix-it, you've got plumbing skills, you're a carpenter? You haven't even fixed your side gate or the screen door."

"Your stove is electric. The coils turn red when they get hot. Somebody probably just knocked the plug out."

"Yeah, and what if you're wrong? We could all suffocate in our sleep. The gas company's there right now, checking it out. The only time they show up is when you tell them there's a leak, then they come, even if it's eleven o'clock at night."

He wasn't sure if Mimi was starting to become a serious attention-getter or if all the kids were driving her blood pressure up high enough to bake her brain. He'd seen it happen to guys on the force. Sharp, first-rate cops who, after having two or three children in short order, started falling asleep on the job, couldn't remember the call numbers, started cleaning their guns without checking to see if they were loaded.

The tiny details, the proliferation of minor annoyances, those were the ones that clogged your arteries and got you in the end. He still didn't know if her brood helped put things into perspective or just knocked them farther out of whack. He'd always fully expected to sit down one day and make a concerted effort to figure it out.

"Put Joan on," he said.

"She had to go talk to Stevie's principal, about the fighting. I told you."

"It's almost midnight."

"It was parent-teacher night, and then the P.T.A. had to have a special assembly about the situation, and then they have coffee and donuts. To them teachers, this is a big night out."

Crease said, "This the same thing or did he get in trouble again?"

"Again. He's shoving kids around. He knocked a girl down in the playground."

"A girl? Why?"

"He says he didn't like the way she was looking at him. She was six, he's eight. The school considers that sort of thing to be a serious matter. It doesn't take much for them to be scared about a lawsuit. A little girl gets her tooth broken or a bloody nose and you'll have a fleet of lawyers on your back. The school has a zero tolerance policy about violence. He might have to transfer." Mimi had shifted gears, she was sharp again, in asskicking mode.

"All kids get into fights."

"He's big for his age and knocking the crap out of six-year-old girls doesn't endear him to the faculty, you know? This is the age of Columbine. What do you think, Crease? You think maybe he's got some problems that need to be worked out?"

"Everyone does."

"Don't get flippant. Not when it comes to your own son."

"You're right, I shouldn't be. I'm sorry. I wanted to speak with him."

"Then you shouldn't have called at twelve o'clock at night. He's asleep, or pretending to be. He might be at his bedroom door, listening in. He does that, if you didn't know. When the phone rings. He's trying to get an edge, taking it all in. Joan will be home in half an hour. Call back then."

"I'll try."

"You settling up what needs to be settled wherever you are?"

"Little by little."

"Work it out faster and come home."

He hung up and a half hour later decided it would be a waste of time trying to talk to Joan or Stevie over the phone. Mimi had been right. He shouldn't have called so late, thinking he could just chat with his boy. He was in denial. Funny to realize it like this. In Hangtree he was maudlin as hell listening to Oldies with tears in his eyes, too scared to talk to his own kid and help him down the right road. He couldn't do it over the phone. Stevie would snarl and grunt and Joan would hum and sigh.

She truly did love him. Like Sarah Burke had said, The truth of love is that you accept what's wrong and ugly and stupid and tainted in your lover. Joan could do that, and it drove Crease berserk.

He really wanted to talk to longshoreman Lenny. He thought maybe Lenny had jumped in the East River just to throw everybody off his scent. He might be out there somewhere with a new name. He wanted to ask Lenny how his life had shaped up, if he'd done anything interesting with it. If he'd become a Hollywood stuntman, a missionary in Pago Pago, or an underwater demolitions expert. Or if he just had another wife somewhere with another brood of children. If he'd gotten it right the second time around. He could see Lenny in front of the tube with his eyes swirling, kids running in front of him, a dog barking, the new wife complaining about the broken dishwasher, wondering how the hell he'd been sucked into it again.

He thought of Morena and wondered if she'd still want him after he'd killed Tucco—if he could kill Tucco. And want him as a husband and a father to the baby, or if they were better off on the sneak, the way things had been for the past two years.

He drifted for a minute thinking about it. Seeing her so beautiful in the morning light that she cooled his burn, as she moved in front of the window with the view of the water, the breeze taking her hair, the skein of sweat dappling her naked skin, her brown skin shadowed by cloud cover. The way she looked when they were in a cab together, headed crosstown to catch a Truffaut revival. Her hair knotted back, her hand in his, discussing European cinema. The two of them chattering like college kids who'd just walked out of class. It gave him hope that there was a life beyond the life.

Yeah, everybody had problems they needed to work out. Jesus.

In the morning he checked out and saw a fifteen dollar charge for some X-rated flick. He vaguely remembered seeing skin on the tube. The bill said he'd ordered it at four a.m. He'd been on autopilot, feverish.

The 'Stang was full of bodies. He felt them in the back seat staring at the back of his head. Thanking him, wishing him further pain, wanting him to hit a bridge. The ghosts piled up, and they still wanted a lot from you.

He hit triple digits getting back to Hangtree, hoping the state patrol would fire up after him, but no cruiser did.

He pulled up in front of Reb's place about noon. He had no idea why he was still staying with her. He should've gotten another motel room, gotten away from her, but there was something so familiar about the house and his connection to it that it grounded him despite all the distractions.

The sad shape of the place, which had bothered him at first, was beginning to become appealing. The collapsed, swaying rain gutters beat out a slow rhythm in time with his pulse. The smell of oncoming rain was strong on the day. He could almost see himself creeping up to Reb's window again, slipping in and out of darkness. The tug of sorrow was still there, and he appreciated its depth.

He was using Reb and a lingering shame had settled in his chest although he'd never made any promises. Even a bent cop didn't have to be bent all the time, in all things.

He walked in and heard her cursing in the kitchen. The stink of ammonia burned his nostrils. She was mopping a floor that hadn't been cleaned in Christ knew how long. She'd kicked over the bucket. A black and yellow puddle of suds rippled against the tile and sluiced up to the baseboards. Dead insects and rat droppings floated along. She was playing house for him again, and doing about as good a job as she'd done with the steaks. He knew it was his own fault.

She said, "If you're going to ask why I'm doing this, let me tell you."

"I wasn't going to ask."

"It's not for you. I'm going to sell this place. I'm going to leave. Maybe you could help out around here a little. Get a hammer and saw and some two by fours out of the shed and fix that hole in the porch, reinforce the stairs."

"Sure."

"There's a chainsaw in the garage you could use on that dead maple. Fix that screen door."

Another broken screen door. Why were screen doors coming down all around him?

"Okay," he said.

"And don't get it in your head that I'm looking for a husband. I'm not. I already know your views on marriage anyway, right? If I did want a husband, it wouldn't be you, right?"

"Right."

She was mad he hadn't come back here last night. He could see it in her face. She'd put him up, fed him, and treated him well as an investment. His staying away all night was evidence that she wasn't going to earn out.

He went out to the garage and got Reb's father's toolbox. He wasn't a carpenter, Mimi had been right about that, but maybe he could get the screen door on. He spent an hour straightening the frame, replacing stripped screws, tightening the spring, and hanging the door back up in place. It had a slight tilt and still didn't completely close, but he figured he'd done a pretty good job of it.

There were three chainsaws under the workbench, but none had gas in them. He couldn't find a gas can anywhere. He drove into town, hit a station, bought a five-gallon jug, had it filled, and got to work filling all three chainsaws. It wasn't until he had them out side by side that he realized they were different sizes. Crease drew out the longest one, fired it up, and got to work on cutting up the maple. He didn't know what the hell he was doing. It took him twenty-five minutes to figure out how to cut v-wedges to keep the saw from getting stuck in the wood. There was sawdust everywhere.

One of the neighbors was burning leaves. The smell grew stronger as the wind burst against his damp neck. The thick aroma drew some good memories forward from when he was a kid, watching his father work in the yard. Wanting to be like the man, like all men of Hangtree, standing tall with their adult mysteries, powerful arms, and faces like flint.

A strange, cold feeling passed over him. His vision blurred for an instant and it took a second to refocus. If he'd married Reb, and moved in with her, and took over her old man's house after his death, and spent years battling the bottle and his own ineptness, he might have wound up here doing this very same thing anyway.

He stacked the cordwood on the back stoop and thought it might be nice to have a fire tonight. He'd have to check the flue and see if it was clean enough to burn logs without smoking them out of the house.

There was no way he could fix the hole in the porch, but he did manage to use some of the cut two by fours in the corner of the garage to reinforce the stairs. He stood there holding the hammer, nails in his teeth, wood chips and sawdust in his hair, and a small rush of pride went through him. Not because he'd managed to spend a few hours filling out Reb's father's shoes, but because he realized that this wasn't the life for him and he hadn't made a bad choice in the first place.

Reb was at the screen door, trying it out. She looked at him and said, "It doesn't close right. I can't lock it."

"Who are you trying to keep out?"

"Jesus freaks and kids selling magazine sub-scriptions."

"That's why I left the hole in the porch."

She didn't laugh. She wore a face that said she'd never laugh again. "Why'd you stack the wood in back?"

"It's getting cooler, feels like rain. I thought it might be nice to have a fire."

"There's squirrel nests in the chimney. Come inside for lunch, if you're hungry."

He put all the tools away and closed the garage and thought the home improvement chapter of his life had now been firmly shut. He walked inside and the cloying smell of detergent made him gag. He went around opening windows while she said behind him, "Is it bad? I didn't notice after the first half hour."

"It's pretty bad."

It took a while but eventually the smell thinned. The place was cleaned up and looked much better than before. Maybe she was serious about selling. Perhaps she could get a good price for the house. You never knew when something was really quaint and when it was tobacco road.

She'd made a tuna salad and had set the dining room table again, but the candles weren't lit. They ate in silence. When he was almost finished he said, "Thank you," and wondered why he hadn't said it earlier.

"What are you thinking about?" Reb asked.

He hadn't been thinking of anything, but for some reason the name was on his lips. "Ellie Groell."

"Ellie Groell? Her? Why?"

"Her shadow was the last thing I saw of this town when I left it."

"Jeez, that's creepy."

No, it wasn't. It was pleasant. He'd been lonely and frightened and looking up at the Groell house had given him a sense of support. He didn't know why. It was getting a little ridiculous, the amount of things that he didn't quite understand.

"She still lives with her grandmother," Reb said. "The two of them alone in that big house. At least I think the grandmother is still alive. I could be wrong, she might be dead."

Reb cleared the table and when she sat down again she had a glass and one of Jimmy Devlin's stolen bottles of Jack Daniels in front of her. She didn't offer him any. Sipping the whiskey got her quietly moaning with a deep pleasure, her eyes closed. When she opened them, she focused on him and said, "Tell me what you've found out so far. About this thing that you came back here for. You discover that your old man didn't shoot the girl?"

"That's never been an issue. I know he did it. He told me so himself with nearly his last breath."

"Then why's any of the rest of it matter, really? I mean, if this is about your father."

"Maybe it's not about him, or not entirely."

"You been talking to your wife?"

That seemed to be a switch in subjects, but maybe it wasn't. Since he'd been back, everything had become even more snarled together. "I've been keeping in touch with my sister-in-law."

"The one with all the kids. Your kids. You talk to her but not your wife?"

"I've called Joan, too, but she's never there."

"Maybe she's got a new man. You said she deserved better."

"She does, but it's not a man."

"How can you be sure? You walked out and it's been a couple of years, right?"

He thought of Joan with another man and, though it made sense, he just couldn't bring himself to believe it. She'd stuck by him through so much already no matter how hard he tried to push her away. Her love was real, it had meaning even if he couldn't return it in full. He looked down at his hands and recalled, one instance after another, all the evil he had done with them, and knew he could never put them on Joan again without wanting to die.

"What about the money? You find out where your father hid it yet?"

She hadn't even asked if he'd figured out who'd kidnapped Mary Burke. The girl wasn't really a part of it, just the cash. She was even more bent than him. "I told you, if he'd taken the money, he wouldn't have snuffed it a drunk in the gutter. Somebody else nabbed it."

"You still planning on killing Edwards?"

"I don't think so. I had a chance the other day. He had one to kill me too, and he didn't."

"Maybe you've both just got other things on your mind. Like you and the bad guy partner. A friend of mine saw you on Main Street with some characters. In a Rolls Royce." She couldn't keep the excitement out of her voice.

"It was a Bentley."

"That belong to your dealer buddy? Did he finally sniff you out all the way up here?"

He didn't like the way she said it. "Would that friend be Jimmy Devlin?"

"No," she said, "it was somebody else."

So she was still working Jimmy, had maybe even set him on Crease again along with the other Jimmys. What did she think that would earn her? Did she hope he'd get hurt so she could nurse him the way he'd taken care of her? Tighten the bond between them. Was that her play? To win him over, take her back to New York with him?

"Don't be too star-struck with fancy cars."

"Why not?"

"Police impound them all, sooner or later."

"Then you just go get another one. Isn't that how it happens?"

"The guys with two hundred grand in a briefcase under their beds are usually the cheapest sons of bitches there are. They're stressed all the time about spending the money. They're more worried about the IRS than they are the feds."

"The smart ones figure their way around that, right?"

"Sometimes."

Crease was going to tell her about Tucco and his whores, some of the things the guy did to the women that got on his nerves or didn't bring in enough cash. Where his business rivals wound up deep-sixed and knife-juked and glass-choked.

Except he knew that's what she wanted to hear. That it was all part of her dream, the hope that she might be able to grab a piece of that action, no matter the cost. She was more like Crease than he'd given her credit for. She'd been working her own edge. Maybe that's why he stayed with her, maybe he'd picked up on it that first night back when he saw her blood on the women's room door.

Call it what you will, she had her own style and was making her own fun.

He'd botched it. He'd thought he was helping her, but really, he was just keeping himself locked and loaded. He'd never be able to warn her off now. Anything he said would just pique her even more.

"A Rolls Royce," she said. "How much have you got put away, Crease?"

"Not much."

It was the wrong thing to say, he was losing his cool again. Even though it was the truth, she wouldn't buy it. Her eyes were whirling like numbers on a slot machine. He'd been pushing the wrong buttons on her. Yeah, the big money came in, but it went out just as fast. The life cost. The more you made the more it took.

She was falling back to type. He was worse for her than Jimmy Devlin or anybody else. He'd put the fear and the need back into her, and saw in the eagerness of her eyes that the coiled energy tamped down within her was going to break soon.

He should get out. He never should've come here in the first place, and now he had to go.

Before he could move she slid in close, the red hair burning in front of his eyes, and said, "I'll do right by you, Crease. Better than your wife. I'll be good to you." She licked her plump lips and raised her chin, turning her head, coming in for a kiss.

"You wouldn't know how, Reb," he told her.

She snapped her head back as if he'd backhanded her. "That's a damn crude thing to say!"

She was right, it was. He said, "I'm sorry," and was surprised that he actually meant it. "I really am. I've got to go."

"What? Go where?"

"I'm leaving, Reb. Thanks for everything."

"Did you just tell me thanks? Thanks, that's all? Is that what you fucking said to me?"

"Goodbye, Reb."

He stood and got his jacket on, reached for the pack and realized he was finally out of those menthols, thank Christ. He turned to ask her if she had a cigarette and caught a dark blur of motion in his peripheral vision.

Shit, he wasn't on his toes.

He started to wheel about faster. His hands were already moving before he fully realized what he was seeing, but it was already too late. Goddamn, you couldn't relax in the game for a minute. Reb was coming around with the candlestick. He would've laughed if he'd had the time, but he didn't. A candlestick. He'd seen people get their heads cracked a lot of ways, but this would be a first. It was a movie moment, something out of a drive-in. She connected and he felt a wide arc of his blood leaving him. He whirled and hit the wall. He let out a chuckle because he knew this was about the fifteen grand. He couldn't blame her. She was too small-minded to realize how short a stash that was, how few bills it paid, how it could hardly get your ass out of debt. He was mad he'd put the time into fixing the screen door, chopping up the tree. He felt a brief, sudden wash of pity for Reb, who in another life might've been his girl. He staggered two steps and didn't get anywhere near her. Then she hit him again and he didn't feel sorry for her at all anymore.

13

The hands were taken care of, felt like cuffs.

His arms were behind him, around a chair. A thin spike of agony rammed through the top of his skull down through the top of his jaw. The spike was made of voices and colors jacked up beyond understanding. Lightning blitzkrieged him with every beat of his pulse.

He'd been here before in this position. It wasn't something you expected to go through more than once in your life, but he figured this was around number three or four. You really had to be looking for it to have it happen so often.

There was somebody close to him but he couldn't focus his eyes. Dried blood on the side of his face pulled his skin taut. That strange sense of duality filled him again. The two versions of himself were drifting side by side. The cop and the crook. It filled him with a wave of joy and loathing.

He heard rain against the windows. Reb's voice came from somewhere across the room. "He's awake." She sounded slightly worried, knowing she was heading into new territory she'd never be able to return from, but excited about it. He'd made this happen.

He blinked but still couldn't distinguish who was right in front of him, the face right there, two inches away. The breath stank of beer, but everybody's in this town did, you couldn't narrow down the list that way. He tried to shake his head and the pain rushed through him again and he had to clench his teeth against it.

Then somebody rapped his head. The jolt rang bells but got his blood humming. He waited for another smack and when it came he started to feel a little better. The copper taste flooded his mouth. It got him thinking straight again.

Reb said, "Don't hurt him anymore."

"Shut up, let me handle this."

"You can handle it, I just don't want you—"

"I said to shut up."

"Don't talk to me that way."

It was Edwards so up close, sitting in another dining room chair. Staring into Crease's face like he was trying to figure out the best way to break a nose in as many pieces as it would go. Ten years later, Crease was beginning to have some second thoughts about punching Edwards out back then.

But the sheriff didn't do anything else. Just sat there studying Crease, really looking at him hard. Hoping to find some answers of his own. Crease realized the guy was thinking about his own duality. Where he'd be if not for that shot in the nose ruining his looks. If only the old man hadn't disheartened him so badly. If only he'd busted the 'nappers all those years ago and bought his way into heroism.

Edwards' features were rigid and he was smiling just a touch and his eyes were eddying with the force of his own fantasies.

You've got a guy here climbing over the hill of middle age, too wide in the belt, a house filled with photos of women who didn't love him. Crease knew the expression well. It was pure, distilled disappointment.

Good, Crease could work with that. The ones who just wanted to chop you to pieces you couldn't out-talk, couldn't really wrangle with. But the ones who wanted the stash, the goods, the talk, those you could keep on the hook at least for a while.

Still, Crease wasn't thinking too clearly. He might have it all jumbled up.

The women around Edwards' house, he thought he remembered that Reb was one of them. Maybe they still had a thing going. That would explain the current situation.

"Where's the money?" Reb said. "Ask about the money. Get him to tell you—"

"If I have to tell you to shut up one more time I'm gonna knock your front teeth out."

"They're already fake," she said.

Edwards turned back to Crease and once more examined him closely. He would see Crease's father in there, see some of the same weaknesses and a few similar strengths.

But the bigtime bend, Edwards wouldn't have any way to recognize that. It would keep him puzzled, a little off-balance.

"I ran your plates," the sheriff said. "You've got a whole new identity. There's a rap sheet on you. You're a pretty bad boy."

"Undercover," he said.

"That's what he told me," Reb said. "Like I was saying to you."

Edwards ignored her, talking to Crease like they were the only two people in the world right now, which they were.

"Undercover narc? You guys are the dirtiest ones on the job."

"Yeah," Crease admitted.

"You were seen in a Bentley owned by a known felon yesterday."

A known felon. Edwards was about forty years out of date with his rap. Tucco had never even been arrested, had never had a felony charge hung on him. Never spent a night in lock-up. Crease had done spurts from a weekend to four months. A known felon, oh yeah.

"You going to ask me a question?" Crease asked.

Edwards couldn't quite make the decision to get tough. He'd been shamed in his own home. Not just getting punched out, but not using the gun when he could've. Crease had seen him too scared to even make a move. That threw you off your stride. It was the kind of thing that blew your gasket after a couple of hours, made you question every action. Crease owned his heart.

"You smuggling drugs into my county?" Edwards asked. He didn't wait for an answer. "Over the Canadian border? What are you bringing down? Untaxed cigarettes? Whiskey?"

"Would you want me to?"

"Depends on my cut."

Crease let out a laugh.

"I want to know what you've got stewing. I want to know why you're here."

"I already told you."

"You didn't tell me anything."

"You weren't listening."

"The hell I wasn't."

You could go around like this all day long. "Okay, you got me. We're not bringing drugs in but we are thinking of knocking over some llama farms. They go for top dollar in Jersey."

"Still being wise."

The chair wasn't that sturdy. Without the spike in his brain Crease could've busted free of it pretty easily, but his hands just weren't doing what they were supposed to be right now. Edwards drew his fist back and slugged Crease squarely in the mouth. It was a pretty nice shot. Crease spit blood on the floor and Reb went, "Ugh, disgusting!"

Edwards said, "You'd better start telling me what I want to know."

Crease knew he could ride it out in the chair for a while longer, long enough to get his hands back, but he really wanted to know why the sheriff's department, including his father, had botched the Burke investigation.

Edwards got him by his front hair and tugged his chin back, ready to take another poke. Crease asked, "Didn't you check into the sister?"

"What?"

"The sister."

"What sister?"

"Burke's sister. Sarah. The girl's aunt. Living with the family at the time."

"Who's going to clean up my floor?" Reb wailed. "He stained my grandmother's throw rug. Goddamn it!"

Edwards let Crease go and turned to glare at Reb, like he might sock her too. His mind was taking him back. It took him a minute to remember. "The spinster? We ran a check on her."

"And didn't turn up anything?"

"No."

"Nothing suspicious at all?" Crease swallowed a mouthful of blood. He didn't want to lose Edwards' attention. The hot splash down his throat got his heart rate stepped up a notch. "No boyfriend with a gambling problem?"

"No."

"How about later, after they put Sarah Burke away? That tell you anything?"

"She broke down. If you're really a cop then you've seen it before. They were a close family."

"You ever listen to yourself talk or do you just hear a loud hum?"

Edwards slapped him with an open hand. It didn't even make Crease's head move. You slap a guy cuffed to a chair like that in front of your boys and you'd never live it down.

"She's in an outpatient home in Langdaff," he said. "The Sinclair Mayridge Home for the Needful. I visited her last night. She's crazy, but not as crazy as she wants to be. She's just got nothing to live for."

"You're lying," Edwards said. It was almost a question.

"Her gambler boyfriend, guy named Daniel Purvis. He's got to be dead, but check on him anyway." Crease's gaze locked with the sheriff's. They were down to it now. "You had so much on your plate at the time, with my father and the department investigation, and you being pissed off at him, that you let the case slip."

"No, that's not how it happened."

"You're an idiot. You should come to New York, you'd be running my department in no time."

Edwards slapped him again, harder. That was better. Crease started to feel the heat working through him. He let out another laugh. His scalp tightened and began to crawl. His upper lip began to bead. The dried blood on his face loosened.

"Stop hitting him!" Reb shouted.

Funny since she was the one who nearly caved in his head, but you took sympathy wherever you could find it.

"Where's the money? Crease, tell him!"

"He doesn't have it," Edwards shouted. "His old man stole it years ago."

"That's not what he said! He said his father tried to take it and—"

"Shut up, Rebecca!"

"Well, get him to talk!"

"A minute ago you didn't want me to hit him, and now—"

"I want that money. Do what you have to do! Or I will!"

"So help me I'll break your head, Reb!"

Edwards was getting twitchy, but really it was Reb you had to worry about. She was the one who wanted it more, and thought Crease was the way to get it.

Crease watched them arguing like a couple that's been married twenty years. They seemed made for each other. The two of them going back and forth about the measly cash. Reb started complaining that she could use the money to fix the place up and Edwards began yelling about Jimmy Devlin and her other dalliances. He actually used the word *dalliances*. It wasn't a word you ever expected to hear when you were cuffed to a chair, but there it was.

Crease picked up another sound too.

It was the subtle clack of the tilted screen door hitting the jamb. But the front door was locked. Crease strained to listen. He wasn't sure if he heard plodding footsteps going around to the back or was only imagining them. The whiff of rain strengthened. The pain in his skull lingered.

Whoever it was knocked over the stack of cordwood Crease had put out back. It wasn't loud enough for Reb and Edwards to quit snapping at each other. They had to burn out soon. They were just hissing like cats now, going on and on about past circumstances. Reb's bad cooking, the sheriff drinking too much to make it in bed. Crease shifted in the chair a bit and was able to see through the kitchen to the back door.

Cruez had slipped his leash. He was trying to make it inside, acting like a sneaky second-story cat burglar. He could barely fit through the door. He let out a soft grunt as he bumped into the jutting metal cabinet with the flour and sugar jars on it.

These people, jazzed up, jonesing, and jinxed to the max, but they didn't hear size sixteen feet come clomping in the kitchen. Crease swallowed down a groan of frustration. He wasn't sure how best to play this turn. Try to snap Edwards' attention back to the moment or look over at Cruez to see what he was after, maybe get him to help out here for a second. You could never tell with somebody like Cruez if the guy wanted bloodshed or just a pat on the head and a T-bone.

From this angle, Cruez could only see Crease, couldn't look at the rest of the room where Edwards was now pouting and Reb was ramping herself up to do much nastier things to Crease than she'd done when they were teenagers. He shouldn't have put down her cooking.

Cruez swept his eyes across Crease in the chair, not quite smart enough to put the whole scene together. All he saw was the target, didn't notice the blood on Crease's face, the way his arms were drawn back. Like this was how he might be relaxing on any weeknight. Jesus.

So it was obvious Cruez hadn't even taken the time to peek in a window. He'd just marched around the house thinking he was slick, expecting to find Crease and Reb settled in for the night. Out on the couch or upstairs in a knotted tangle. A smile started to cross his rough, lumpy face and got lost in crazy ways among the scarred features.

"I'm the right hand," he said and started to pull his Magnum.

Okay, so that answered that question.

Crease shouted, "Sheriff, this man wants to smuggle llamas over the Canadian border! Arrest him! I'll take the stand against him!"

Edwards was still wrapped up inside his own head but when Cruez's shadow preceded him out into the dining room, and Edwards got a gander of the behemoth extracting that long, way goddamn long-barreled .357, he got back in cop mode fast.

He hopped up and ran forward as Cruez broke completely from the darkness of the kitchen. Edwards whispered, "Christ."

Cruez's expression contorted and his facial muscles ground together into a frown. "We didn't see any llamas. We saw cows."

The front sight of the Magnum had snagged on the bottom of his shoulder holster. That was another reason not to carry the damn things, no holster was long enough to hold them properly.

Reb did the best thing she could've done under the circumstances. With Crease sitting there bleeding, the sheriff failing to come up with the fifteen g's, now some piece of a mountain climbing into her house, she just cut loose. It was weird, definitely proving she had some schizoid tendencies of her own. She let out a wickedly eerie laugh that sent the creeps up Crease's spine.

It was a titter tinged with desperation, guilt, fear, and the underlying wish to take everything back from the last twenty years or so.

Good thing Edwards was ready to shoot somebody this time. He pulled his gun and pressed the barrel of his .38 on Cruez's Adam's apple and shoved hard.

It was a move that would've put a normal guy down, but Cruez was wired differently. His thoughts banged around inside that skull and became blunt and lost all their force. He didn't feel pain like other people. He was still yanking at the Magnum.

Edwards said, "That what you planning to do, you llama thief? You go to hell, Canadian!"

Rebecca's cackle had died down but was still sputtering at the back of her throat. She looked drunk, out of it.

Crease said, "Reb, the keys, okay?"

"I don't know where they are!"

"They're right there on the table."

Edwards had a little more steel and sand to him than Crease had thought. The sheriff didn't want to just blow Cruez away. He stood his ground. He thumped the monolith in the throat again, and then pistol-whipped him. Three, four, five times, the .38 coming down hard across Cruez's nose, his chin, his forehead. Spatters of blood whipped against the wall. Cruez was still reaching, and now the barrel was finally starting to come free.

Crease was this close to letting out that cackle himself. His cool was mostly gone, but sometimes the coolest thing you could do was get off a chuckle at the right time.

Reb fumbled for the handcuff keys. She wasn't going to get to him in time. The sheriff had played it wrong, he shouldn't have tried to chip away at Cruez. He could've bashed the guy in the head with a shovel all day long and not left a dent.

Cruez, the moron, could've easily swatted the sheriff aside but he was too intent on drawing his weapon. He wasn't exactly the most adaptable guy in the world.

Yeah, that laugh, everybody made it now and again. There always came a time when you had a *what the hell* moment of clarity and realized just how ridiculous your life had made you. Like him yelling about llamas.

Oh yeah, you had to laugh.

Crease's hands were starting to do their thing. They were pulling at the back of the chair and the wood had begun to splinter, cracking as loudly as rifle shots. The chair gave out and Crease went with it, hit the floor and tucked himself in tight, working his arms down around his thighs, his legs, his shoes. Cruez was bringing the Magnum out while Edwards continued to clobber him.

Crease's bundle was on the table. His gun, the butterfly blade, the Bowie knife. He got his cuffed arms all the way around and out in front of him and jumped to his feet. He wasn't sure he was going to be fast enough. His hands were flashing out, the left taking the Bowie, the right the pistol. Cruez had the Magnum out but Edwards was too close to him, he couldn't quite get it pointed the right way. The sheriff finally realized he'd made a mistake and turned his own gun around in his hand, ready to blast Cruez. But the butt was slippery with blood and he couldn't get a good enough grip on it.

And here you were thinking today that a fire would be nice. Some wine, the smell of fall wafting in around you.

Crease tapped the point of the Bowie against the back of Edwards' hand hard enough to make him drop his slick gun. Crease gestured him away towards the couch. Then he pushed the .38 against Cruez's crotch and said, "Okay, that's enough, let's settle down now."

"What?"

That was about as much as you were going to get out of Cruez at a time like this.

"Talk to me. Why are you here?"

"I'm not left-handed."

"I know that," Crease said. But he realized Cruez was trying to tell him more but couldn't find the words. The eyes in that bloody, misshapen head looked like holes poked into clay with a stick.

"Tucco know you're here?"

"No."

"How's Morena?"

"What?"

"How is she?"

"Bored."

"What do you want?"

The blood coated his face looking like somebody had used a roller to go straight up the middle of it. "I'm not left-handed!"

Crease said, "You're the right hand. That's okay, everybody knows you're the right hand. You're Tucco's man. His best man."

"Yes."

"You're the top dog, the big cheese, right? Not me, you. You're the honcho. You're the prince of good fortune, the duke of the deal."

Cruez's shoulders hitched as he took a deep staggered breath. For a moment he appeared to be a very large deformed child who had climbed a neighbor's fence to get his ball and couldn't find it anywhere. You never knew what was going to defuse a situation. A little extra cash, a line of coke, a well-timed joke. Whatever it took, it was usually better than the alternative.

"Tomorrow," Cruez said, walking out the front door. Crease knew what was going to happen next and wanted to shout about it. Cruez shoved and swung the screen door opened so hard that it collapsed off its hinges. He said, "Tucco and me, we'll see you then."

Reb was standing there in the center of the living room, arms crossed across her chest, grasping her elbows. Crease saw her again the way he had the other day, for the first time in ten years, with her storm-blown hair sweeping across her throat, her fiery eyes full of anger and faint dignity. She was taking a stand because it was all she had left. She wasn't about to run or try to make a grab for Edwards' gun on the dining room floor. That scam was over, and she'd missed the train.

She said, "Crease, I'm sorry."

She meant it, as much as she was able. "I still need the keys, Reb, all right?"

The sheriff was sitting on the couch. He'd grabbed the wine on his way over and was drinking from the bottle, a little out of sorts. Reb got the keys and uncuffed him, her and Edwards trying not to act like they'd just been smacking him around a few minutes ago. Maybe the sheriff knew he'd been out of his league tonight. Crease was from a different world now.

"He really gonna bring llamas down from Canada?" Edwards asked. "Probably loaded with dope, right? That's how they do it? Open 'em up and stuff in the balloons and then stitch them back up again."

"From what I see, you two are about perfect for each other. How about if you just tie the knot and let everything else drift away, huh?"

"I asked," Edwards said. "She told me no."

"I didn't tell you no," Reb said. "I just wanted more time. I said to let me think about it."

"It's been fourteen months. If you've got to think about it more than a day or two, the answer is no."

"You asked three other women to marry you the same year. So how serious were you?"

"Very," he said, not sounding very serious about anything at all. Right then, Crease saw so much of his old man in Edwards that he had to draw the back of his hand across his eyes just to shake off the vision.

Crease told the sheriff, "The sister, go send someone to talk to her. You won't even have to shake it out of her. Just show up and she'll spill everything."

He put his gun in its holster, got his jacket on and put the knives back in his pockets. Reb floated up behind him. Her breath on his neck did nothing to him. She put a hand on his wrist in some kind of display that neither of them would ever understand. He turned and spotted his dried splashes of blood on the corridor wall and thought it was just as well that he was getting the hell out of here.

The powerful feeling that time was running out filled him with an electric rush of trepidation. Both he and Tucco had reached the end of their patience. Still, he had one last thing he had to figure out.

Edwards took a long look, pulled a face, and shook his head. "What the hell are you all about?"

Crease said, "A guy who makes jigsaw puzzle dogs to hang on the wall is gonna ask me that?"

14

When you didn't know what to do, where else did you go?

Only one place left that mattered. You went to visit your father's grave.

The one good thing about having the old man die in such shame, covered in vomit, in the gutter, the town shunning him, is that Crease never got the feeling that his father was judging him. Whatever wrong Crease did, however crazy or stupid he got, the old man's ghost wasn't about to point a finger. Sometimes that didn't mean anything, sometimes it was all that mattered.

He parked and found his way to his father's grave again, each step somehow riling him, the pressure building. He had to finish up this thing with the little girl's death, and then he could settle down to finishing matters with Tucco. Despite the events of the last couple days, his resolve still seemed to be waning.

The awareness of his own inadequacies really was annoying the hell out of him. He wondered if, given the same circumstances, the same facts and conditions and respective positions, his father could've figured out what had happened to the money. He was having more and more trouble imagining his old man in his prime. Strong, fit, sharp, before the liquor and sorrow and his own fear wore him down into a pudgy, wet sack.

The old man's grave, which had been sunken in the last time Crease visited, had now been restored by Dirtwater. New sod had replaced the patchy yellow grass. The large round rocks had been reformed into a kind of small cairn, surrounded by fresh flowers. The largest rock was on top, and painted on it in a child's handwriting was his father's name embellished with a picture of a yellow sun and a bird and smiling kid walking a dog.

A small wave of sentimentality swept through Crease's chest. He started for Dirtwater's small house but before he was halfway there, he saw the caretaker and his son raking graves in the distance. He altered course and when the boy, Hale, spotted him, he waved. Crease waved back. The kid touched his father on the elbow and Dirtwater turned and grinned.

Crease said to them, "Thanks for fixing up the grave, I appreciate it."

Hale said, "Your face, you've been fighting. Who did that to you, if you don't mind me asking?"

"I don't. It was the sheriff."

"My father hates him."

"Yeah."

"My father says you're the one who broke his nose, is that true?"

"It is."

"Was he paying you back for that?"

"For that and some other things."

Dirtwater's gestures grew much clearer to Crease as the man shadowboxed and gave Crease the thumbs up. "He wants to know if you got some good licks in."

"Not today, but I did knock him down a few times yesterday."

"He's glad. So am I."

Hale searched Crease's eyes. The kid had a great sensitivity to body language and expression, thanks to his father. "You know something about the girl, don't you? Something you didn't know the last time you were here." Eight years old and his acumen was on the money. Crease got a good vibe from the kid, but still it was spooky. For an undercover narc, the worst person you could run into was somebody who could read your face as easily as this kid could.

Dirtwater's dark eyes showed a dogged interest. He made an "out with it" gesture and Crease didn't quite know what to say.

So he knew who the 'nappers were. It didn't change anything. Nothing was going to happen to the old broad at this date, with her in assisted living. The insanity plea would actually work in her case and she'd get sent right back to where she was now anyway. He could only hope every criminal he ran into would have such a case of conscience that they locked themselves away.

He halfway hoped that Dirtwater had somehow stolen the cash. There was a certain balance to that. His only friend left in town, the man who cared for his father's grave. The money could've gone to a down payment for his house. Cello lessons for Hale. A college fund, special medication he needed. A kidney transplant. Crease was bushed thinking about who else's hand might be in the jar. It could be anybody. Cruez's entrance today reinforced the fact that you couldn't shove Tucco out on the rim for too long before he got tired of being pushed. The rest of the questions surrounding Mary Burke might have to take a back seat, forever.

"He says you look like you need a glass of whiskey."

"I don't drink," Crease said.

"He says he didn't know that, but maybe you need something. Some food? My mother made a roasted chicken last night, there's still some left."

Crease still hadn't met Dirtwater's wife, didn't even know her name. She might be someone he'd once known well, she might have had a great impact on his life. But the thread that connected them was too tenuous and he'd never find out for sure.

"You want to see her grave again, don't you?"

"Yeah, I think I do." He didn't know why, except he felt the road coming to an end and he thought he'd get just as much out of spending time standing over her grave as standing over his father's.

Dirtwater and his boy walked side by side with Crease. He felt Dirtwater's intense inner strength again. It defined the man even more than his face and body did. How many shovelfuls of dirt had he pulled out of graves and then stuck back in? Laid out end to end he'd probably dug enough earth to take him to the west coast. He didn't know much about the man at all, but at the moment Crease felt very much like the gravedigger might be his only friend in the world.

Dirtwater put a powerful hand on Crease's back and patted his shoulder. It was somehow an action that reminded Crease of his father, even though his father had never done it to him. Dirtwater's deeply expressive gaze told him volumes about love and loss and the desolation of the dead. The gravedigger cocked his chin towards his house, mimicked drinking, trying to get Crease to come along for a couple of beers.

"He wants you to—"

"I know, but I don't think I can today."

"Why not?"

"Something's gnawing at me and it won't stop."

"What is it?"

"That's a good question, kid. I hope to find an answer in the next couple of hours."

Hale nodded sagely, and so did Dirtwater, both of them ancient in their ways and manners because being a part of the dead didn't have to wear you down.

Crease followed Dirtwater and the boy, doing his best to move like them, wafting between headstones, skipping over roots. The man's power drawing him along.

They came to Mary Burke's grave again. Hale had placed fresh flowers on it.

"You did nice, Hale."

"Thank you."

No matter where you went you always came back. They stood like that for a while again. Sam Burke had been unable to face the truth, and had sacrificed himself to his perpetual lie. Her aunt was dying by inches afraid of light. Reb had betrayed him for loot she could make herself on a good weekend in Tucco's club. The wind's sad whistling drew Crease's attention across the cemetery.

"You think she's happy?" Hale asked.

It must've been a subject that wasn't supposed to be breached, because Dirtwater placed his hands firmly on his son's shoulders, shook his head at the boy.

"He doesn't like me asking questions like that. It upsets some people. I ask about heaven and God and if dead people are awake or sleeping. I can't help it. I can't help thinking things like that. My mother says it's because little boys aren't supposed to be around death all the time."

"It's not that," Crease said. "It's just that nobody has any of the answers, and they usually don't like to be reminded."

"You don't mind, do you?"

"No. I've been around a lot of death too. I've been curious on occasion."

"He says he can still see your sadness, but there's something else to it."

Like you didn't have enough on your mind, the kid had to just keep on spooking you.

"He says you're getting back to who you're supposed to be."

"That so?"

"It is."

"Maybe he's right. Maybe not."

Crease stared into the boy's eyes, seeing the child he was in there. You could witness a lot in Dirtwater's face, and you could see as much, maybe even more, in his son's. The whispers of the wind made him turn his face aside, wondering what his old man would have him do now. Give up and run for it? Ambush Tucco while he was asleep in Morena's arms? Dirtwater stepped up, as if knowing Crease's thoughts and wanting, in some way, to take the place of his father. It could get on your nerves, all this silence.

"You know what happened to her?"

"Mostly."

"Maybe that'll make her happy."

"I don't see how."

"He says that maybe you're thinking about it in the wrong way."

Crease figured that was probably true. "Okay, so how should I think about it?"

He kept his eyes on Dirtwater while the man spoke to his son in a language that wasn't language. He kept his eyes on him even while the boy talked. "You know who did it?"

"Yeah."

"You know why?"

"Yeah."

"What's left to learn then?"

"What happened to the money."

"Does that matter now?"

"Only because it caused all the trouble in the first place. It was my father's destruction. I'd like to find it and burn it, if I could. But I don't know who stole it."

Some mysteries you're not meant to answer. Some of them are supposed to continue on and on, marking your life.

"He says maybe somebody didn't steal the money. Maybe something else happened to it."

"What else could happen to it?"

"He doesn't know that, he's just offering a suggestion."

There would never be an end to this for him if he couldn't track the last piece of the mystery. He wouldn't be able to face Tucco with his head clear and his hand ready, not with the little dead girl in his back seat and Teddy hissing in his ear. The goddamn fifteen grand would be his finish too.

15

Five hours she'd had on the loose.

He'd made an understandable mistake. He hadn't gone far enough when he was play-acting around here before. He'd stepped into his drunk father's shoes and imagined himself being Edwards at the door, but he hadn't thought enough about the girl.

Six years old.

Your aunt lets you off at the far end of the abandoned mill, tells you to shoo. Gives you a little push.

A six-year-old, you don't realize how sharp they are at first. They constantly surprise you—how much they hear, how much they know that you never expected them to pick up.

Mary Burke would've heard her aunt and Purvis discussing the cash. How important it was to them, how much they needed it to get out of debt, make the guys who'd taken Purvis' leg leave them alone once and for all. On the drive up to the mill they were probably laughing, talking about resettling somewhere, raising a family of their own. While Mary was in the back taking it all in, knowing that her aunt had just traded her in. For what, Teddy? Why is this happening? For some short green, Mary, that's the truth of love.

You're six years old. Teddy's giving you good advice but it isn't enough. You see your aunt walking away, getting back in the car. She's angry, there's something that's upset their plans.

Would you walk into a deserted mill, no matter what she'd told you? Hell no. You'd follow your aunt.

He saw Sarah Burke and Daniel Purvis getting into their car and pulling away onto the logging trail, heading back to town. Mary would start running after them, maybe crying.

You race along the trail for as long as you can, but soon you tire and the car is long gone. The forest is terrifying in its dark implications. You're alone and wailing and Teddy's abruptly gone silent.

What do you do, even if you are a smart six-year-old? You're still a baby. You hunch down and sob, waiting for somebody to come find and help you. Where are Mommy and Daddy?

Teddy mutters, Don't rely on them, you're on your own.

It's been a rough day. You've learned a lot about life and your family. Your aunt is a liar who loves only, entirely, another person. Your father and mother cannot protect you. Teddy really doesn't know so much and he's got a mean streak. These lessons would wear anyone out.

You hide and you take a nap. It's the thing you do when you are angry. When your face is covered with hot tears. You find a small warm spot to curl away in.

Even a happy child can fall into a state of depression. Let's say a half hour following the trail, a couple hours of bitter, dreamless sleep in the woods, wedged between two logs, using Teddy as a pillow.

When you awake, you're disoriented, but you don't cry anymore. You've been transformed by your new world view. Teddy is jazzed up again and really chattering away. You hug him close and start back along the trail the way you've come. Another half hour.

You stand outside the mill. You see a man in the woods but you don't trust him. There's no reason for you to. He's crouched behind weeds, his handsome face is marred by self-interest. Aunt Sarah told you to walk inside and you'd be found. You don't believe her, but you haven't got many options left. You're tired and hungry. So's Teddy, and he's really bending your ear about it.

You are quiet. You like to play hide-and-seek. Your father is not here to use his commanding voice to draw you from the niches and nooks of the house. You can be in charge of the game.

So it goes like this. Your body is at ease in the shadows. There are great bulks of machinery strewn about in the long, wide room.

The man inside is asleep, or almost so. There's something wrong with him. He mumbles in his sleep and he shakes. You silently slip around him, hoping for a better view. He is a policeman. Your father has told you to trust such men, but your father may have been lying too. He failed in his duty. He and mother are at home eating ice cream and giving presents to each other, glad to be done with you. Your anger swells. Teddy snarls evil words in your ear.

There are spoked metal wheels with little cars on wires. There is money on the floor beneath them. Cash, Teddy says, there's the damn cash. It looks like the policeman tried to hide the bundles of bills, but some have slipped out, there is green paper sticking up.

You would hide behind the track that wheels ran on. You would crawl. You want the money because everyone else wants the money. Maybe you can show it to your aunt and then yank it away while she reaches for it. You'll laugh in her face. You will be able to buy many friends with the money and your friends will beat up your aunt and that man and your parents. Your friends will throw many hard things at them and your parents will cry and beg forgiveness and you'll laugh at them also.

Teddy tells you to do it. Go on, be careful, grab the cash, baby.

You carefully reach out into the wheels. It's easy, your hands are small. You stick the bills in your shirt until you're all puffed out with a big fat belly. You slide back to where there's a hole in the wall and you slip through it and quietly walk into the bushes. You leave the mill behind. The money is heavier than you expected it to be. You're dirty and sweaty and the paper sticks to your skin under your shirt. It's a warm day, you're very thirsty.

You know what you will do. You'll hide the money and then go back and demand the policeman take you somewhere safe, and for that you will pay him later. You'll come back and pick up the bills and you and Teddy will give him some of them.

Teddy goes, I like the plan, all cops are bent. They'll sell their mothers for a wad of stash.

You creep back into the mill through the hole, ready to approach the policeman. His hands are shaking. He's nervous or sick about something, probably because they don't pay him enough. She'll pay him and he will be her friend.

The door opens and the other policeman enters with his gun coming up and Teddy goes, Oh shit.

Crease snapped himself out of it. His heart was clattering in his chest and his pulse ticked so heavily in his throat that it felt like Tucco was tapping the point of a butterfly blade against his neck. Salt stung his eyes and it took a minute to settle down, get Teddy's voice out of his head. Jesus.

He turned and looked behind him and there was the hole that a little girl could've crawled through carrying a couple of short stacks of bills. Fifteen thousand, what his father thought would save him, spirited off by a six-year-old and a stuffed bear.

He moved out from behind the carriage of the trimmer and walked to the rusted flatbed with the bent spoked wheels and cut cables. The broad opening where the slabs of wood would be hauled down the incline led to a two story drop over an embankment. She couldn't have gone that way.

But down at the nearest corner rotted flooring disclosed the crawlspace area beneath the decking. It was large enough for him to climb down into. Seventeen years ago, it would've been smaller, and might've been overlooked by everyone but an angry kid looking to settle a score.

He went out to the 'Stang, found a flashlight in his trunk. It surprised him that it was there, and that the batteries still worked. Except for the spare and a jack, you never found what you needed in the trunk when you needed it.

One time, when a deal had gone sour in an apartment building in the south Bronx, Crease had seen a guy hurl himself into a wall thinking he was going to crash right through. Big guy, went maybe two-fifty of gut, but he had it in his mind he could work up enough momentum to bust out the other side. Get into the next apartment and make a run for it. Crease and Tucco watched the guy smash himself again and again into the wall—which did crack a little, a few paint chips spurting off—while the guy mashed his ribs and busted his face. It got surreal after a while, the guy trying to dig through the sheetrock. Tucco and Crease were enthralled watching him, and finally it was Cruez who came up with his Magnum and put the guy through the wall once and for all.

Crease thought of that scene as he worked to enlarge the hole, kicking out some of the flooring. It took him twenty minutes before he could really climb down, carefully maneuvering himself along the joists and beams and cement foundation built into the side of the hill.

Daylight dappled the groundwork base and rodents squeaked and rasped as he made his way down. There was hardly any need for the flashlight as he braced himself and moved from board to board. He saw Mary Burke doing the same thing, laughing as Teddy spurred her on, thinking about how her family would learn the hard lessons. The bundles under her shirt fattening her up, the bills soft but cold against her skin.

The belly of the building, this was the best place to hide.

He hit bottom and saw, by the sweeping rays of light, a clear path through which he could exit. He shined the flash around and knew Teddy would be extra sharp even now, telling Mary what to do. He'd want her to hide it, just in case.

Lots of hidey holes between the timbers. Crease hunched down, looking up, seeing this place the way someone smaller would. He let the urge to be hidden begin to overwhelm him. He wanted to stay in the shadows, allow them to twist about him and what he had brought into them. Teddy's voice would be loud under the mill, every squeak exaggerated a hundredfold.

Mary had things to do. She wouldn't be able to go with her impulse to play, to enjoy the darkness. Six years old and already so strong. What kind of a woman would she have become?

The timbers and joists and cinderblocks all looked the same. She wouldn't want to stray far. She'd need to find the money again for when she used it to reign over her family.

Bent over, Crease backed up and put his hand out where the first two beams crossed leaving a V-shaped open ledge. He touched paper. His fingertips were electrified and actually pained him. He shined the flashlight down on the area and saw red eyes reflected back at him. He instinctively snapped back as squeals retreated to the distant corners. He reached into the spot again and pulled out wads of rat-eaten, water-soaked, disintegrating bills.

The reason for the girl's death.

After Mary had hidden the cash she'd walked back out around the bottom of the foundation, up the incline to the far end of the mill, and in through the open side where Sarah Burke had originally given Mary the little push to go on. The girl had walked between his drunken father and the greedy deputy busting in the front door, the two guys gunning for each other.

The last thing she would've heard was Teddy going, Oh shit. She'd have hugged him closer and maybe closed her eyes an instant before—

Crease sat in the darkness, feverish. He wanted to kill somebody, but everyone who mattered was already dead.

It didn't take much to get you believing in fate.

Thinking your life was wrapped around somebody else's that you hardly even knew. For years the thread connecting you wouldn't be noticed, and then one day it started to tug and you got reeled in.

He pulled out the clumps of money and the shredded bills crumbled to pieces in his hands. He took off his jacket and threw the decaying paper in. The stacks were even smaller than he'd imagined they would be. A lot of the cash had been torn up and dragged off for nests. He knotted the sleeves together, threw the bundle over his shoulder, and climbed back up out of the hole into the mill. He went out the front door and got in the 'Stang and stomped the pedal, throwing mud everywhere.

Finding the cash wouldn't allow his old man or Mary to rest any easier. He couldn't even give it to Reb to show her how little it was. Finding the cash just didn't mean a damn thing.

He never should have come back to Hangtree. He should've marched down to the club where Tucco and Cruez were in the back getting lap dances, walked into the place and shot them both in the face. He would've got his medal and gone on from there.

16

But at least it was done.

He drove over to the sheriff's office, parked, walked in with the bundle, and saw Edwards at his desk in back. Edwards spotted him coming and started shouting orders to the deputies, who all looked terrified at getting yelled at. You could tell it wasn't that kind of police station. Nobody laid a hand on him.

Crease unknotted his jacket, threw the decaying cash on Edwards' desk, and said, "Here it is."

"Here what is?"

"Mary took it herself. Her own ransom. She was a smart kid. She knew what was going down. She hid it under the mill."

Edwards' expression went from joyful surprise to complete despair in half a second. "This isn't money."

"Yeah, it is."

He looked closer. "No it's not, it's some kind of clothing, isn't it? But—"

"Modern paper cash isn't so much paper as it is cloth. That's what's left of it. After rain and mudslides and rats and birds have been at it. You never searched the mill?"

"We searched all over it, the grounds, everyplace."

"But not under it?"

He sat and picked up some of the wads, trying to piece them together. "I don't remember. Yeah, we must've. Most of it. Some of it."

In other words, no. "You put in a call to the Sinclair Mayridge Home for the Needful?"

"Yeah. Sarah Burke died this morning. She'd swiped somebody else's medication. Turns out she was allergic. She must've been taking the wrong pills for a while. Weeks. That's the only thing that lets you off the hook, in case you were wondering."

Crease nodded. "The right meds wouldn't have helped anyway. It went down the way she wanted it to."

"You talk like nothing matters to you, you know that? That an act, or do you really not care?"

You had to let some things slide. "Make sure you tell Sam Burke. He needs to know about this soon, so he can find himself in the mirror again."

"What?"

"Just tell him."

"Sure. Of course. What's this about a mirror?"

"Forget it." Crease turned to go but the words were out of his mouth before he could stop himself. "What happened to Teddy?"

"Who the hell is Teddy?"

"The bear."

"What bear?"

"Mary's doll. The one she was holding when she got capped."

Edwards stared at Crease like he couldn't believe what he saw. "How the hell should I know? What are you talking about now?"

He wasn't sure. Out of everything, it was Teddy that had somehow gotten under his skin.

Sneering, Edwards threw down a handful of the clumped, dusty bills and a cloud rose around his head. "You still think this is all I cared about, don't you."

"It doesn't matter—" Crease said, and he realized Edwards was right. He really did go through the world like nothing mattered to him at all. How much worse off did that put him than the rest of the mooks?

"You think I shot her. That's what you've been back here for. You want me to admit I did it. But I didn't. It was your old man."

"I always thought it was."

"You want me to confess."

"Confess to who?"

He stared at Edwards trying to see the man and not see his father, but it was just too difficult keeping them separated now. This had been his father's office, his father's chair. That wet, round alcoholic face was looking more and more like his old man every minute. He wanted to crack him across the nose again or maybe just shake his hand, get it out of his damn system once and for all. He hated the sheriff with the same deep, relentless, meaningless fury he'd reserved for his father. He felt it swarming up inside him once more. Crease struggled to tamp it back down.

"You finish up with that big son of a bitch yet?"

"You heard him. Tomorrow."

"Good. Don't let me know where. Keep it out of town."

"Why don't you ask Reb to marry you again?"

"What?"

"You've got nothing to lose."

"You of all people is gonna say that to me? She nearly caved your head in for a bird's nest. She's crazy!"

Crease shrugged. "Maybe you two can work it out. You make a good couple. Really."

"You're crazy too," the sheriff said, his breath thick with wine. No longer golden or handsome, his hand trembling with the need for more drink. The women in his house were ready for him, his puzzle dog was waiting. "Now go on and get yourself shot. Do it close to a gutter so no one has to clean up after you."

Crease thought it was a pretty good line. *Close to the gutter.* He didn't think Edwards had it in him, but anybody could fire off a lucky one. He found another motel and spent the night practicing with the knife, working out some kinks, getting his head as clear as he could. He settled into a deep, mostly dreamless sleep punctuated by Teddy giving him advice on the drug trade, telling him who he should wipe out next to widen his hold. You had to wonder when the bear was becoming your new best friend.

In the morning he called Morena's cell. "Where are you?"

"Driving around, looking at boys' schools."

"What road?"

"Who knows? I think we're lost. We've been searching for the llamas. That was some goddamn comment you made. You started him on this whole thing to find llamas. He's obsessed with it. Every morning, seven a.m., we leave the motel and go looking for the llamas all day. He's bought seven of those big bulky sweaters." Her voice shifted, grew very tight and hard. "He killed an old woman."

"What?"

"Because you told him not to. I think she was a teacher at one of the military academies. Maybe a nurse or just somebody's mother, I don't know. She was walking across the parking lot and Cruez pulled up slow. Tucco asked for directions to the llama farm. I thought he was serious. Then he pulled his knife and stuck it in her head, jabbed it through her temple. I didn't have any time to warn her."

A shard of ice worked against Crease's neck before turning to fire. The voice became even more ancient, like another ten thousand years had been piled into it. "Are you okay?"

"I'm wishing you hadn't decided to come back to this place, you know? I really think you were stupid to warn him the way you did, playing cowboy. You starting to pick up on that yet?"

"Yeah." She was right, but he couldn't change anything now. He had to ride it out to the end. "Put him on."

"He's sitting across from me, pretending to be asleep. I guess that means he doesn't want to talk to you."

Pretending to be asleep to avoid conversation, the same thing Stevie did. "Tell Cruez to figure out his way back to town. I'll meet you on the outskirts, right before the highway. There's a pull-off there, he'll see it."

"You're being dumb again," she said. "You shouldn't play it out like this. Haven't you learned anything?"

He supposed not. "Does it matter? Just tell him."

"You want to die, don't you? It doesn't have to be that way. You can make a better choice."

"Don't you worry about me, baby."

There was a moment of silence and then a very brief sigh, like Morena didn't want to waste any more breath on him. "You saying that makes me worry most of all."

The Bentley pulled up and slid in beside the 'Stang at one-thirty. Cruez must've really been off the map or else Tucco wanted Crease to wait, just so it felt like he was the one calling the shots. Crease was leaning against the driver's door, his .38 on the hood in plain sight. Tucco got out of the back wearing a black llama wool sweater that looked three sizes too big. It swallowed him.

Man, one off the cuff comment and you could regret it forever. A woman, dead, because of Crease's big mouth. Morena had been right about everything, and yet Crease felt himself caught in the riptide, being dragged along with no way to stop himself.

"We looked, man," Tucco told him, "but we didn't find any llamas."

"Forget it."

"You sure they got farms? Like, they milk them things? The cowboys, they rope them? Run 'em across the country in llama drives, like cattle? Them we saw, the cows. Lots of cows up here. I think Cruez fell in love with one. He likes their eyes, you know? On a woman it's sexy, but we're talking cows here. He can't tell the difference. They got skiing. You didn't mention skiing."

"I've never been skiing."

"Those boarding schools, these military kids . . . after they learn all about rifles, becoming snipers, if it was me, first thing I'd do after graduation, I'd go home and waste my parents for sticking me in there."

Morena said, "He's been talking like that for two days. This is what you did to him."

Crease nodded. He knew what it meant. Tucco was feverish. He'd taken a lot and enjoyed how far out on the rim he was standing, but now he'd been pushed far enough and was about to make his move.

"You shouldn't have snuffed the old lady," Crease said.

"Since when do you care who I ice and who I don't?"

"Since you did it just to get back at me."

Tucco grinned, barely showing his teeth, talking out the side of his mouth like he had a large audience. "Now he's sensitive. Now the badge means something to him. Before, he'd cap anybody, clip 'em three, four at a time. How many wild shots do you think went out the window, killed some baby in a crib across the way? Just so you could bust some seventeen-year-old Colombian mule, throw 'em into prison forever?"

It was happening to Crease too, the feeling of being so far out on the edge there was nothing beneath him anymore.

Maybe that's why they'd become friends. Because once you found a player as good as you were you really didn't want to beat him, you just wanted the game to go on and on.

"You can't hurt me," Tucco said. "No matter how many old ladies I waste. You tried to hurt me and you couldn't do it. Nobody wanted to hear. You put a gun in my face and couldn't pull the trigger. How long we been together, huh? Two years?"

"Little more."

"All that time you haven't hurt my business, haven't even put away any of my best guys."

"I know," Crease said softly.

"The coke keeps flowing, the pills, the H, the ladies do what they do, the johns are happy. The money keeps coming in. Got more girls on the street now than ever. You've cleaned up my messes, taken out my competition. I'm worth twice now what I was two years ago, maybe three times. You've made me what I am."

"Don't say that."

"It's true."

"That doesn't matter."

Tucco was hitting his stride. "Of course it matters. It's all that matters. You know that."

The back of Cruez's right hand gleamed with gun oil. Crease knew that he could walk right up to the monster and shoot him in the heart and Tucco would just smile about it, shake his head like it was a good joke. Nobody meant anything to him except maybe Crease, which made it all the worse.

"Come back with me, man," Tucco said. "I need you. I can't trust anybody else. They all got secrets. But you, you don't have any secrets now. I know you, all of you, inside and out. Loco bastard like you, we work on the same level. We need the same things. That's what I need in my partner. Just come on back."

"I can't."

Tucco waited. "Well, why not?"

"I'm not sure."

He waited some more. "That's it, that's all you're going to say? You're not sure? That's it?"

Like it was easy, putting your life into words. Your contradictions, your guilt, your jones. Nobody else could understand what it was like carrying your old man on your back for seven years, loving him and hating him, sending your will into his heart hoping it would stop beating, for his sake. How much you could care about your wife and son and yet despise the position they put you in. To be the middle-class mook, the guy picking out wallpaper, trimming the lawn, reading fairy tales, going over the times tables. Anything that took you off the point of the knife just wasn't ever going to be good enough.

But so was going back to where he'd been with Tucco. It just wasn't possible. The engine had been screaming for too long. Even if you couldn't take the curve, you had to stomp the pedal and keep your weight on it. You had to.

"That's it," Crease said.

Tucco was going for the butterfly blade.

He knew Tucco had already started going for the knife even though he couldn't actually see him moving. Tucco was speeding along in his brain, willing it to happen. Nobody had shifted an inch and already Crease was being outmaneuvered.

Too slow, he almost let loose with a laugh. His hands started going for the blade but he was too slow, he'd lost a lot of his frosty competence screwing around with Edwards and the Jimmys. Crease had known it was coming and it still didn't matter. Even if you were a step ahead, sometimes that wasn't enough.

He couldn't help himself. His gaze shifted to Morena. He wanted to look at her, fill himself with a touch of her beauty, a little of his longing. Still trying to decide if they could really love each other. It was another mistake. He realized it at once but her eyes confirmed it. They didn't show any fright or even alarm. He could see the regret there, the dissatisfaction. Even a touch of pity.

He was surprised that he felt so cold. Jesus Christ, he was freezing. Where was the heat now that he needed it? His blood wasn't moving.

Tucco stepped in, his blade still not showing. Crease almost had his out. It was going to be close but not close enough. Crease stabbed forward a fraction of a second before Tucco completed his move. A surge of pride went through him.

It ended almost instantly. He'd gotten there first but all he'd cut was that fucking llama sweater. He'd missed.

Tucco's knife slid into Crease's stomach just above his bellybutton. It went in and in and Crease just watched it.

He didn't hurt yet. He'd already gone into shock. He dropped back and drew himself off the blade and leaned back up against the 'Stang.

The end of the game. The bop till you drop contest over. Tucco looked extremely sad, like he didn't want to do it but, maybe, this was the kindest thing for them all. He took another step forward, got ready to bring the knife in again.

Morena was near Crease but not next to him. He wondered what the hell that meant. He saw her glide away, her black hair roiling in the sunlight like liquid, as she spun to him. The shadowed curves of her body revived him for a second. He felt strong and righteous.

Then her hand was coming up, just a blur.

She was faster than Crease, faster than Tucco. Her eyes reflected nothing.

Tucco said, "Goddamn, woman."

She eased the barrel of Crease's .38 against the back of Tucco's head, pulled the trigger, and blew his brains into the middle of the road.

She said, "You idiots and your knives."

Crease angled his chin at Cruez, worried about the monolith moving in. "What about him?"

"What about him? He works for us now." She pocketed his gun. "Did you expect it to be any different?" She held his jacket open and inspected the wound, the blood leaking steadily down his pants. She unwrapped a wool scarf and tied it around his waist, pulled it tight. "Come on, we need to get you to a hospital. It's not that bad. You'll be all right."

He stared at her and thought, This is my woman. This is the woman for me.

It was a good thing she didn't lie or he might be worried. She helped him to the Bentley. Cruez got in behind the wheel. He hadn't said a word this whole time and didn't need to. He was doing the only thing he could, being the right hand. Morena opened the back door and Crease looked in but couldn't climb inside.

He turned back and stared at Tucco's corpse on the ground, wondering where he was supposed to go from here.

"Don't," Morena said. "Don't run. Stay with me."

"I'm not running."

"You are, you're backing up. You're going to run. Don't go."

"I'm not," he told her. But he felt himself moving away from her and couldn't seem to stop.

"You don't really want to die, do you?" she asked.

"I don't know," he said.

"Just come with me. I'll take care of you."

"You wouldn't know how," he said.

"Come home. Everything will be okay now."

He was terrified she might be right. They'd walk away together now and he'd . . . what? Go back to being a cop, shine his badge up again, put his father's back on the mantel. Or take over the business, run it the way it should be run. There was a list of about five guys that, if he popped them all, most of the tri-state area would be his. He could do either. Marry Morena. Raise the kid as a punk who would know the street from minute one. Or maybe a boy in blue, like Stevie was, attending PBA events and waving in the parade. He wondered if he could even quote Miranda anymore. He was torn up the middle.

"Think about the baby," Morena said. It was the most emotional she could sound, but she didn't sound emotional at all. "Your child."

He backed up some more and hit the hood of the 'Stang. He turned over and left a thin blood trail across the headlight. He got into the car. He pulled a rag from beneath the seat, carefully drew back the scarf, and jammed the rag into the wound. Tucco's blade had been so sharp that the incision was extremely clean and things still weren't hurting. There was hardly any bleeding now that he'd plugged the hole.

He turned the car around. Morena's eyes followed him in the rearview.

He gunned it for the highway and changed his mind, doubled back, wanted to see Hangtree one last time. He tore up Main Street and circled the city. Crease hit the outskirts of town ripping seventy down neighborhood streets. He was spinning his wheels like always.

As he was about to pass the Groell place he plunged down on the brake. The 'Stang skidded and sluiced to the side, the smoke billowing from the squealing tires. Old lady Virginny must be dead, the window that he'd come to think of as *hers* was empty.

But in the other one, the one that was Ellie's, he saw movement behind the shade. It was the same as when he'd left last time.

Maybe he was already dead and damned to repeat these same ludicrous motions forever. Her silhouette seemed to wag its wrist at him, waving goodbye. The house might be empty, shared by ghosts. He had always been one with the shadows. He had to be crazy.

He slapped it back into gear and headed for New York.

Home.

17

Teddy taunted him. Crease didn't mind much. The voice kept him awake.

So he was nuts. There was no other way to explain why he didn't rush to a hospital instead of driving to New York. You had to live with some truths and die with others. The entire ride he considered his options, if he should happen to make it. He could tell the whole story to his superiors and get reassigned to some other dealer or runner. Spend another couple of years on the rim, climbing up the chain and getting in tight with somebody just like Tucco, eventually have another showdown. He could do that.

Teddy was telling him to just give in and go with the cash flow. Morena would help him make it work. They could just take over the business, improve holdings. Tucco had been lazy, hadn't expanded when he should have, allowed too many people to skim. It wouldn't be like that anymore.

When they sent in another narc, Crease should be able to sniff the guy out easily. And even if he couldn't, they wouldn't care about taking him down so long as he gave a few others up along the way.

He took I-91 south through Massachusetts and crossed over into Connecticut. Pockets of intense rain swept across the road like it was clearing half the world away. He wanted to go with it. The sun broke through. I-95 was loaded with family trailers and SUVs and elderly couples out for a New England Drive.

The dead were packed into the 'Stang with him. They whispered loudly and he tried his best to listen, to their advice or confessions, but their chatter drowned each other out. Mary was telling Teddy to shut up. There still wasn't any pain. The wound had stopped bleeding and Morena's scarf made a decent bandage.

Morena had his gun and he'd left his own butterfly blade stuck in Tucco's sweater, but he still had the Bowie, in case he needed it. He didn't know why it comforted him. The dead razzed him about it. Teddy said he was sexually hung up. Mary Burke tried to strangle the bear but she didn't have any luck. Teddy kept on talking.

Crease hit New York and swung it out across the Throgs Neck onto Long Island just as the sun began to set.

He couldn't remember the last time he'd been to his own house. He didn't fully understand why he was back now. Maybe to fix the screen door. Maybe to ask forgiveness from Stevie.

It was possible. He thought of laying side by side with Joan in their bed and a part of him wanted to let loose with a groan of relief and another part knew it could never work. Her bringing him breakfast in bed. Her calling out to him in the bathroom saying he needed to remember to floss. Her asking all the time, What are you thinking?

The tires squealed as he took the exit too fast, muscling through traffic on the service road until he finally turned into the neighborhood. He let the 'Stang prowl, low-slung and growling as it paced up and down the blocks. Teddy told him to get ready for a surprise.

There was a Taurus just pulling away from the curb in front of the house. Crease caught a flash of a mustached face and shiny moussed hair before the guy slid past and was gone around the corner.

Crease pulled into the driveway and got out. His legs were shaky and a wave of nausea rolled over him, but it was over in a moment. He buttoned his jacket. He got to the door and wasn't sure what to do. He should probably knock, but this was his house. The house of the cop he was, that he used to be. His father told him to walk in. Crease walked in.

Joan was in the living room, bent over the coffee table clearing away an empty bottle of beer, a half-finished screwdriver, and a bowl of chips and salsa. He checked his watch. Seven o'clock. An after work drink with the guy.

Well, he thought. Well.

He smelled fresh-baked pie. From a back room—Stevie's room—came the throb of music. He started down the hall and stopped. He still didn't know what the hell he might say to his son.

Joan stepped over and said, "You don't look well. Your face, you've been fighting. Are you all right?"

"Yeah."

"Do you need something?"

"I don't know."

"Why are you here?"

He never expected her to ask why. All this time, he'd figured she'd just take him back, feed him meals, swab his wounds, talk his ear off until he hated her. She said, "Crease? Talk to me. What's happened? What's wrong?" She noticed the pants, where his blood had darkened them. "What's all over you?"

He stared into her eyes and he didn't hate her at all. It was a revelation of sorts.

"Who was that?" he asked.

"A friend."

"A friend," he repeated. "Your friend?"

"His name is Ken. He's very nice. He's a guidance counselor at Stevie's school."

So that's where she'd been until midnight after the parent-teacher meeting. And Crease had been telling Reb he was certain that Joan didn't have another man. Out of everything, why had he been so confident about that?

"Crease, why are you walking like that? Are you drunk? Are you sick? Did you throw up on yourself? Tell me what you want me to do."

"Nothing," he said.

"Then why are you here?"

"I want to see Stevie."

Her face hardened. She checked down the hall to see if their son's door was still closed. "I don't think that would be such a good idea."

Crease couldn't believe what he'd heard. "What?"

"Ken says that Stevie has a great deal of repressed rage towards you."

"It's not so repressed."

"All the more reason why, if you're serious about dealing with some issues, we should be in counseling."

He almost agreed. "Joan, I just want to see him for a minute, all right? Then I'll go."

"What do you want to say to him?"

"I won't know until I say it."

The roar of an engine broke the night, swarming the house until the windows rattled. The mad screech of tires tore up the street. Crease parted the blinds. Jesus Christ, it was the Bentley. Sure, if the tech kids could find him in Hangtree, they could find him here.

He had choices to make, and the sense that time was running out filled him with a flood of anxiety. Odd, when you thought about it, since Tucco was now dead. One war was over. Maybe it had been the easiest one to fight. This other one with himself just kept on going and going and would never come to an end.

"Who are those people outside?" Joan asked.

Crease turned and went for Stevie's room, but the door was open. His beautiful boy was standing there staring at him, saying nothing.

He walked to his son. Stevie was afraid and backed up, step by step until he was almost in the kitchen, scowling with his face turning red.

"Stevie?" Crease said. "I just want to talk to you for a minute, okay?"

The boy shook his head, not in response to his father's plea but as if he was trying to deaden noises in his skull. Crease had done it to the kid, passed over his problems. As far as he'd tried to keep away from him, he'd always been close enough to do the wrong thing. The expression on his face was something Crease couldn't put a name to. He knew of no word to cover it. He'd never seen it before, not on anyone. His heart beat savagely in his chest at the thought of what the boy must be going through. He took a step forward and the kid retreated. He took another step and Stevie continued to back away.

"When you were born," he said, "I thought I'd made good in the world. I'm sorry. I expected you to save me somehow. It was wrong of me to put that burden on you."

"Crease!" Joan called. "There are people running up the walk. Who are they? What trouble did you bring to my house?"

The question was, what trouble could he take away? He kept approaching his son and Stevie backed up into the kitchen.

The pie had needed to cool before Joan sliced it, but she must've thought of cutting up a piece for her new boyfriend. Crease could see the guy saying, No no, don't go to any trouble, as she scurried around the kitchen doing what she loved to do best. Treating other people kindly. Being a mother.

The knife was there on the counter and as Crease walked in Stevie went for it.

Knives, always with the knives.

Most people think of an eight-year-old as a baby. Little. Weak. But Stevie had some weight and real muscle to him already, and he was full of intent. He had a lot of rage built up inside him all right, his own fever burning. The kid was sweating. Crease tried to find something to say but everything that ran through his head sounded even more foolish than all the things he'd already said to his son.

Last time he'd tucked Stevie into bed the kid had a teddy bear propped in his arms. Teddy would lean over and look at the pictures with him. Crease would kiss Stevie goodnight and kiss Teddy goodnight too. The boy would giggle and tell him to kiss Teddy again, and Crease would.

Now, Teddy wanted blood, the kid had his vengeance to visit upon his father. The hardshell hadn't taken long to grow on him. How hard was it to read fairy tales to your baby boy? It ought to be natural. If you can blunder that you can blunder anything.

His thoughts were scattershot, winging all over. He thought of how much he had loved his own old man before the downfall. It should be worth something but it wasn't, not a thing. He had a lot to say to Stevie. Warnings, prophecies, suggestions. Guidance. Counsel, cautions, instructions.

He moved in and Stevie lashed out with the knife. The kid was fast. Crease barely got out of the way in time.

He tried again and Stevie tagged him good. The knife ripped through Morena's scarf and stuck into the same place where Tucco had shanked him.

The pain blew out the top of Crease's head.

He couldn't even scream, just let out a deep, choked up yelp. It was the kind of noise you made when your kid pretends to shoot you on the front lawn and you play dead for him.

His father had gutted him when he was a kid, and now his son had done the same thing. There was a nice balance to that, despite the agony. He couldn't help but feel like he deserved it, that the universe just wanted it this way.

Stevie thought he'd done all the damage himself and started to shriek as his father's blood poured onto the kitchen floor. Crease went down, first to one knee, then both. Then he flopped over onto his back.

He looked up at the ceiling and saw that it was stuccoed. He'd lived in the house for almost five years and never realized that.

He'd been wounded in the line of duty two, three times early in his career. It was one of the ways to advance, to collect the medals. He could take some heat, but Stevie had really put the bite on him. Blood and bile pulsed between his fingers as he tightened his hands over the wound.

He realized, with sudden, overdue clarity, that when Morena mentioned being pregnant he should've gone and just busted Tucco and returned home to Joan and Stevie. If for no other reason than to ask their forgiveness, to explain himself as best he could. He should've held his son and fought past the fever, reached the boy with quiet, honest words. Going back to Hangtree, it got him nothing, meant nothing in the end. Funny how you only recognize diversions for what they are when they're over, when you finally see how you've wasted your time.

Joan stepped into the kitchen and started screaming too. Behind her came Morena and Cruez. Joan turned and looked at them and started shouting. It was kind of funny, really, the two worlds colliding. Joan didn't think to call 911. She loved him but she loved being incapable and sorta ditsy even more. She ran in and started hugging Stevie, trying to put her hand over his eyes, the two of them howling. Maybe it should have made Crease feel cherished, but he just wanted them to shut the hell up. She dragged their son to the far side of the kitchen, as far away from Cruez as she could get, cringing from the man-monolith.

Morena stepped in, her face blank, already in charge. She grabbed a dishtowel, leaned over him and pressed it hard against his belly. It hurt like a son of a bitch now, but he liked her hand on him, the fierce power of her body up against his. She'd followed him four hundred miles, riding his tail right to his front door.

"You don't want to die," she said.

"No," he told her, "I don't think I do."

"Hold on."

Maybe it was love, maybe not. Whatever it was, he appreciated having her here now. He tried to hold her close, to put his palm across her belly and feel the baby, but she was moving again.

She shouted at Joan, "Get more towels. Call an ambulance."

"Who are you?" Joan screamed. "What are you doing in my house?"

"Move! We need the towels!"

"Get out of my house!"

Stevie broke from his mother and stepped closer. The kid was pale and panting and sweating. From the floor, Crease held his hand out to his son. The kid stood there crying, which might be a good sign. Crease wanted to tell him to quit picking on the little kids, there was no reason to be shoving girls around, he was going to have a baby brother or sister soon. He had to learn to be nice, to pick his battles, to lay off the weak, to slap down the hoods and degenerates. Stevie stared at him. Cruez came around and started to eat the pie with his fingers, grunting with pleasure. Joan continued whimpering, and she was weaving side to side but she wouldn't come any closer. Morena had snatched up the phone but didn't know the address and she was yelling at Joan to tell her, but Joan wouldn't or couldn't do it. Teddy told him he was finished. Crease made it to his feet and stumbled to the table where he sat heavily. The table had been so white and he was getting it dirty fast. He managed to light a cigarette but felt too tired to even take a drag. He held his hand out to his son again, hoping the boy would take it soon.

About the Author

Tom Piccirilli lives in Colorado where, besides writing, he spends an inordinate amount of time watching trash cult films and reading Gold Medal classic noir and hardboiled novels. He's a fan of Asian cinema, especially horror movies, pinky violence, and samurai flicks. He also likes walking his dogs around the neighborhood. Are you starting to get the hint that he doesn't have a particularly active social life? Well to heck with you, buddy, yours isn't much better. Give him any static and he'll smack you in the mush, dig? Tom also enjoys making new friends. He's the author of seventeen novels including *The Cold Spot*, *The Midnight Road*, *The Dead Letters*, *A Choir of Ill Children*, and *Headstone City*. He's a four-time winner of the Bram Stoker Award and a final nominee for the World Fantasy Award and the International Thriller Writers Award.

To learn more, check out his official website, Epitaphs, at www.tompiccirilli.com.

READ ON

for more intensity and suspense
from Creeping Hemlock Press!

Are you the one who helped him kill the angel?

Twenty years of repressed anger and memories.
A bitter knot of hatred that binds and divides two friends.
The dark secret that fuels and devastates them both.

He killed it. I only helped him to bury it.

by Tom Piccirilli

"I read this in one sitting because it was so original in every aspect
that it left me no choice. I'd discovered literary gold."

> Ed Gorman, author of *The Day the Music
> Died* and co-author of *City of Night* and
> *Dead and Alive* with Dean Koontz

Frayed is only available in a beautiful, limited-edition hardcover state
from Creeping Hemlock Press and other select independent retailers.
Signed and numbered, this fine collectible can grace your bookshelf
for just $35 US. Buyers and dealers alike may contact us and learn
more at our website.

www.creepinghemlock.com

Turn the page to read Chapter One . . .

Gray invited me up to the insane asylum hootenanny.

He said there'd be lots of pretty girls, rich food, and non-alcoholic beer. I'd been struggling with the middle of my novel before he went in the bin, and he figured correctly I'd still be stuck dead in pretty much the same place now, six months later. "It'll do you good," he told me over the phone, sounding happier than I'd heard him in years.

I drove the hour north up the Thruway to the Clinic, expecting to see electrified fences topped with razor wire and gun-toting security guards all over the grounds. Or at the very least lots of burly orderlies in white, carrying truncheons, cans of mace. Grinning and waiting to catch some psychotic climbing down knotted sheets. But the skinny guy reading a supermarket tabloid in the booth at the gate just lifted the semaphore arm and waved me in. No second glance, no crow's feet at his eyes.

At the front desk of the main building I gave my name. A tiny Asian nurse with reams of black hair spilling from beneath her little hat told me that Gray was located in dwelling #4. She handed me a detailed map and made a red X where I was to go. She smiled vacantly at me as if I was a lunatic, and I had the faint impression that the red X might be a booby trap, a pit laid out with sharpened bamboo stakes. It felt very easy to lose control of yourself in a mental hospital because you wouldn't have very far to travel to find a bed.

I walked over to Gray's cottage. It really was a tiny cottage, one of four spaced directly in front of the Olympic-sized pool where several girls were swimming and laughing. They waved at me and I waved back.

The door was open and I stepped in. The place had a Hawaiian motif going, very much like a cabana. He had a large bar with five wooden stools, and there were coconuts, a mini-surfboard, and netting hanging in the corners of the room. The nets were full of papier mâché lobsters with bright blue eyes and broad, smiling faces.

A large L-shaped sofa took up much of the room. Off to one side was an extremely clean kitchenette with a breakfast nook that had a freshly cut rose in a crystal vase sitting on the table. This is the home where you live every night in your dreams, where you are beloved and admired and respected for your talents, and they bow when they bring you the fruity drinks. The bedroom door hung ajar and I spotted the edge of a double bed overflowing with an absurd amount of extravagant pillows.

All in all, the cabana was about three times the size of my apartment in the city.

This is why men climb towers with high-powered rifles. This is why they go to war and learn to hack off ears. Because of this we beat our wives. Brutalize our children. Light ourselves on fire. Simply, small jealousies climb into the back of our skulls, one slimy trail after the other, until they're so densely packed that your thoughts are like sparks thrown from flint striking stone.

Gray sat on the couch facing away from me, typing on

his laptop and absorbed by the process, an unsharpened pencil wedged between his even, white teeth. I stared over his shoulder and read the first two paragraphs of the story he was working on. The work was solid, poetic, and distinctive, everything my own writing wasn't anymore.

He'd lost weight and had a deep, rich tan, as if he'd been digging ditches or graves. Maybe boxing in the outdoor rings the way he had in college. He'd dyed the gray out of his beard, had a sharp stylish haircut, and wore slick, new clothes that fit him well.

So it wasn't bedlam. No serpent pits, iron bars, or strait-jackets. No rubber rooms or medieval torture devices designed to drive evil spirits from the lunatics. A loud splash outside was followed by the flutter of provocative giggles.

"How do I get into this place?" I asked.

He turned, looked up, and spit the pencil out. "Just try to kill someone who's done you wrong," he told me. "And be so conflicted about it that you make at least one fairly dramatic suicide attempt."

"I can probably do that," I said.

"I know you can."

It felt like he wanted to get into a serious talk right now, from the first minute, and start hashing out a few of our many unresolved issues, which probably wouldn't be the best thing to do. I steeled myself in case he came at me—perhaps even wanting him to, willing him to—but he sat back, checked his screen, and corrected a typo. Since there were no doctors or attendants around keeping watch, I had to be the one to act the most casual and anchored, which wasn't a good role for me.

"You look great," I told him. "How do you feel?"

He had to think about it for a while. "Clear-headed," he finally admitted. "For the first time in a very long while. Some of the static seems to have faded, you know?"

I stared out the window. A couple of gorgeous women went by in bikinis, holding froo-froo drinks and magazines. They looked over and caught me watching. They waved again, and I waved back again.

"You sure this is really a mental hospital?"

"More like a preserve. You get to see the wildlife in its natural habitat."

"A cabana is your natural habitat?"

"In the best of all possible worlds I suppose it would be."

He let out a laugh that wasn't a laugh. It was a sound I was familiar with, and there was a tinge of sorrow and hate in it. He was trying to tell me, or himself, something that he couldn't say aloud, so it just circled inside his chest for a time, hunting for a way to get out.

"So this is it? The best world for you?"

"Better than Manhattan."

"Well, yeah."

"You still watering my plants?" he asked, genuinely interested.

"You only have one plant and it's a cactus. It's pretty low-maintenance."

"Unlike the rest of us."

He said it with that strained chuckle once more. He missed his digs. The harsh action of the street, the museums and bookstores, the overbearing weight of history, art, and literature laid across his shoulders, reminding him he was alive. His three ex-wives. The whores he met in the alleys, and the sweethearts he took to the theater. You could become addicted to dichotomy. The nuns and priests who guided his worship. Maybe even me. All the things that had sent him over the big edge in the first place.

I knew better than to ask him about his work. We often clashed on the approach and execution of the writing, the development of style, the procedure of publication. It had been our dream as kids, our passion as teenagers, and our downfall as adults.

But it would be a good way to gauge how the Clinic might be helping Gray to get past his trouble areas, many of which I shared with him. I stepped over to his coffee table and glanced again at the laptop. I saw him jerk as the muscles in his back tightened, but at least he didn't tackle me. That was progress so far as I was concerned.

He struck the chord first and asked, "So why are you

snagged in the latest book?"

"I'm not certain," I said, surprised at how effortlessly I'd answered. What you hold back the most becomes the easiest to part with. "My concentration isn't worth shit nowadays. I can knock out short stories and I've been busy with freelance non-fiction crap, but whenever I try to duck my chin and go in for the long haul, something bounces me out again. It's getting on my nerves, to be honest. I'm pacing the apartment at all hours. My neighbors are starting to put in complaints to the building manager."

"You need to spend more time outside, in the park. People-watch, take some notes. The fresh air will do you good. It might help if you bought yourself a laptop. You're never without a chance to produce."

"I can't compose directly onto those things," I told him. "I can transcribe my handwritten notes, but that's it."

"Don't be so resolute. Give it a try."

The idea of Gray giving me advice, consoling me about my work, made me jerk as the muscles tightened in my back. Man, it took no time at all for the two of us to get under

each other's skin. Sometimes it felt good to have that kind of power in your life, and sometimes you had to ponder why you cared. He put a hand on my shoulder and I looked around at the shining bar top and the little happy lobster faces, wondering if there was any chance I could get a margarita. I sat on one of the stools and thought about how much it was like the small restaurants where our fathers used to drink wine together.

Gray smiled, showing off those perfect teeth again. He'd had some dental work done here too. Jesus, no wonder my taxes were so high. Who the fuck was footing the bill for his vacation?

"How about you?" I asked. "You seem to be back on your stride. What're you working on?"

He'd been thinking about his response since before I'd walked in the door. It rolled off his lips like he'd been practicing his dialogue in front of a mirror. Which he used to do. Which we both used to do. "A supernatural suspense about two brothers who find out they're the sons of a fallen archangel. One follows his father's will to try to destroy the world and the other refuses. They both end up in Jerusalem gathering various biblical artifacts as Armageddon approaches. Monty has the first three chapters and there's interest from three editors. He's trying to drive them into a bidding war."

Monty Stobbs was Gray's agent, a shark in the chum-filled waters of publishing. He'd made Gray a major hit out of the gate ten years ago, and since then Gray had completed five cinderblock-sized novels, and not one was worth a damn. Monty had mishandled my career for a time, and even though I'd made some good cash up front, Monty's deals had screwed me over in my

royalties and reprint rights.

Gray's book actually sounded intriguing and marketable, and from what I'd read of it just now I knew it had some narrative muscle to it. But I couldn't shake the feeling that the publishing world would only be attracted to his book because they could push it as a novel written in a mental hospital. They wouldn't know Gray had cottage #4. They'd play up the electroshock angle, make it seem like he wrote the whole thing with a crayon stuck between his teeth while he was tied down to a bed. Frontal lobe surgery, the sexually heinous acts of deviant attendants. How could it not rocket to #1 on the New York Times bestseller list?

"I'm glad for you," I told him. "You deserve to have them perk up and take notice."

"You're full of shit, but thanks for trying." It was such a left-handed comment that I actually shook my head as if he'd tagged me with a jab. "I appreciate you making the effort to pretend to care about my career." He said it with a tight grin of authority, as if he'd seen through me and found me utterly lacking.

Now that got me pissed, and the familiar heat rushed up into my chest and into my throat. The way he always implied I could never really be happy for him. "I meant it."

"Okay."

"Not only okay . . . I meant what I said."

"You're just repeating yourself now."

"Because I want you to believe me."

"Is that what you want, Eddie?"

"Yes." I held in the thrashing animal. We all had to hold in the thrashing animal, I knew, though I'd forgotten exactly why. Some stupid prick had once thought it was better that way. "Is there some reason why you can't simply accept my good will towards you?"

"Good will?" Gray's smile was little more than a leer. "I see. So that what you call it?"

"What the hell are you going on about now?"

"You figure it out."

"Listen to me, you—!"

A shadow crossed before me. A short, elfin blonde about

twenty-five years old with eager eyes and a cautious smile stood in the entrance to the cottage. Her presence snapped me back into myself and I stepped away from Gray, kind of humbled before her.

She was pretty in the way that we both liked, blonde with freckles, with an innocence in her manner, especially the slightly shy way she didn't meet anyone's gaze dead-on.

My imagination burned like kindling. Showing me images of her and me on a front porch of an old Victorian homestead, drinking lemonade in the summer twilight, waving to neighbors while the kids played inside. It was a stupid, romanticized notion of a life that never was and never could be, but it kept me from giving in whenever the unbearable darkness hit.

She had a girl next door smile even though I lived next door to a bodega on the upper west side.

She said, "Excuse me, Mr. Gray. Will you be coming over to Ward C for the assembly?"

"Yes, Trudy."

"That's wonderful. I made apple fritters, brownies, oatmeal raisin cookies, and devil's food cake. I'm not sure what I should bring. Do you have any preference?"

"No, but I think my friend might."

I tried not to take it as a dig that I'd gained weight while he'd trimmed up. I took a step forward and she did a little dodge, adeptly moving aside. "I've always had a penchant for oatmeal raisin cookies myself," I said.

She smiled bashfully and sort of toed the carpet, then spun and rushed outside again.

Gray pursed his lips and said, "You can crash on the couch, if you like."

"Thanks, maybe I will."

"Or if it makes you uncomfortable being here, there's a motel right outside the Clinic grounds where the families of patients occasionally stay. The town's called Griffinsville. Three stop lights and lots of antique shops for the tourists. Lots of farming back roads. Abundant in small lakes and ponds. It might be the kind of vacation you need. A chance to go fishing."

I glanced through the window again as another lovely young woman in a string bikini walked by. I let out a sigh. I was a very good sigher. I'd had a lot of practice.

The girl Trudy bounded back in. She had the brownies and said, "Let's go, the dance will be starting soon."

I followed them out past the folks playing volleyball in the pool, my mouth watering for everything and nothing.

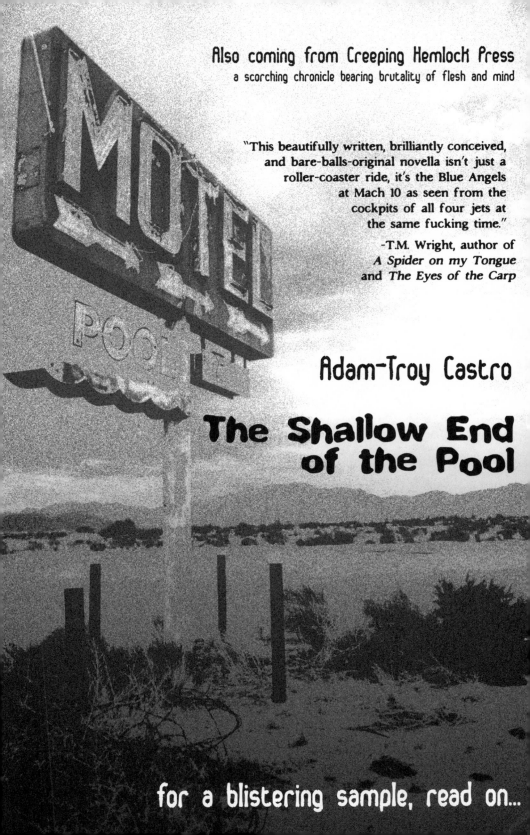

Also coming from Creeping Hemlock Press
a scorching chronicle bearing brutality of flesh and mind

"This beautifully written, brilliantly conceived,
and bare-balls-original novella isn't just a
roller-coaster ride, it's the Blue Angels
at Mach 10 as seen from the
cockpits of all four jets at
the same fucking time."

-T.M. Wright, author of
A Spider on my Tongue
and *The Eyes of the Carp*

Adam-Troy Castro

The Shallow End of the Pool

for a blistering sample, read on...

I had to make another go for him.

Padding along the warm concrete floor of the pool, which had not yet given up all the heat of the day, I made my way toward him, stopping every step or so to keep him from triangulating my position from the sound of my breath. Not that stealth mattered all that much; the thin layer of grit at the bottom of pool made every step crunch like an old-fashioned soft-shoe.

I tried not to think about how big he was and how badly he'd hurt me the last time we'd faced each other.

In my head, he'd grown to twice his actual size.

In my head, he was an ogre, towering over me like any other creature of old fantasies, with arms the size of tree trunks and a head that blotted out the sky. In my head, I only came up to his waist.

An image from an old stop-motion movie intruded, painting Ethan as a roaring Cyclops, scooping up badly-imposed sailors to bite in half with one chomp of his oversized jaws.

I cursed my imagination. This was stupid. He was nothing but a boy: a big, stupid, overdeveloped boy too clumsy for his own good.

Daddy had said, "You're better than him, honey."

He had said, "You'll win as long as you have heart."

He had said, "I have faith in you, Jen."

The Bitch might have said any number of things like that to Ethan, but then, she was the Bitch, and she was used to lies and deceit. Just look at all the things she had done to Daddy.

When Daddy said things like that, he told the truth.

I made it to the line that separated the Deep and Shallow ends. The bowl ahead of me was inkier and, it seemed, deeper than it had any right to be. I couldn't see the far wall, not even in reflection: there was too much shadow there even to admit the distant light of the stars. It was too black to see Ethan, but I could still hear his breathing, somewhere ahead of me: ragged, wet, and labored. It didn't sound like he was lying down. I got the clear impression that he was standing against the far wall, beneath what would have been the diving board, confident in his own ability to meet my advance with a strength that trumped my own.

He was accurate enough there. If he was waiting for me, I should turn back.

I took another step to be sure.

Something nearby smelled like a sewer.

I still couldn't see him. I listened for him and all of a sudden couldn't hear him either.

I couldn't bring myself to hope that he'd died in the last. More likely, he'd realized I was close and was holding his breath and long as he was able, to keep from being able to track him.

That trick worked for two as well as one. I couldn't close my mouth or pinch my nostrils shut, but I held my diaphragm tight and held my next breath as long as I could, counting off the seconds.

Ten. Thirty.

One minute.

I could hold my breath for two.

More, since my life depended on it.

Ninety. Still no sound from him.

He couldn't be dead. I could feel him.

Was he moving toward me?

Coming up on two minutes. My heart was pounding.

Two minutes. Still silence.

Would I even be able to hear him over the roar of the blood in my ears?

Two minutes ten.

corpse blossoms

Ed. Julia & R.J. Sevin

"*Corpse Blossoms* is WONDERFUL!!! Buy it, read it, digest it, share it with all your friends and relations, and all passersby, too."

> T.M. Wright, author of *A Spider on my Tongue*
> and *The Eyes of the Carp*

"*Corpse Blossoms* is the best, most consistently satisfying anthology I've read in years . . . Clearly these stories were chosen for good writing first and foremost over simple shocks, which is refreshing as hell."

> Jack Ketchum, author of *The Girl Next Door*
> and *Off Season*

For original, suspenseful short horror, little in recent years can match the critically acclaimed *Corpse Blossoms*, nominated for the Horror Writers Association's Bram Stoker Award. A weighty, clever anthology, it comprises twenty-four haunting tales from such greats as Bentley Little, Gary A. Braunbeck, Ramsey Campbell, Scott Nicholson and Nick Mamatas. *Corpse Blossoms* is a handsome collectible available from independent booksellers and directly from Creeping Hemlock Press at www.creepinghemlock.com.
$40 unsigned edition, available now - *Limited to 500 copies*
$70 signed and numbered edition, coming Summer 2008 - *Limited to 500 copies*

An excerpt from Tom Piccirilli's "An Average Insanity, A Common Agony"
They thought it was just the funniest thing ever, bringing the old guy *and* his dog into the place. Three college jocks drunker than hell but with a real edge about them, carrying a harsh atmosphere inside with them from the street. Vin tightened in his chair as a flush of heat went through his belly. It only took a glance to know everything about them: a trio of starting line seniors but the pros hadn't come knocking like they were supposed to. Now at twenty-two these kids were already witnessing the fall of their dreams, the slow flat resentment angling up through their lives.

It's why they were so loud. Laughing wildly, easing loose with a little madness, pushing the blind man on, grabbing him roughly and hugging him to their barrel chests as if he were their greatest love. His cane tapped mercilessly, slapping at puddles of spilled beer on the floor. Even the guide dog walked warily beside its master, watchful, sensing a vague evil.

Vin felt it too. His scalp prickled and the sweat began to writhe at his temples.   □

UNTO DUST

TALES OF APOCALYPSE

Creeping Hemlock Press presents a thrilling new collectors' series of novellas to take you to the end of days and beyond. Turn to www.creepinghemlock.com for details on this original project!

VOLUME I: JACK'S MAGIC BEANS
by Brian Keene

In the blink of an eye, the world goes mad. The bestselling author of *The Rising*, *Ghoul*, and *Dead Sea* brings you the shocking chronicle of a common day, a common place, a common psychosis consuming everything in its path. Working against time and terror, the survivors must uncover the truth behind their own immunity. A modern master of splatterpunk has outdone himself with this ferocious and imaginative treat. To be published in three states in March of 2008.

$30—*Unto Dust* edition: limited quantity available from select dealers.
$45—F.U.K.U. edition: Sold Out!
Lettered edition: Limited quantities. Inquire immediately.

VOLUME II: CHILDREN OF THE NEW DISORDER
by Tim Lebbon & Lindy Moore

An age ago, the children stopped coming. The priests' promise of a curative kept the fury at bay. When the airships dropped their antidote, a desperate people drank it up. Marooned and hopeless, Chaylie and her family were spared the horrors that followed, only to return to a land plagued by the tragic and the bizarre.

They appear in the night. Deformed. Mewling. Inhuman. It's Chaylie's job to destroy them in great, blistering heaps. The living nightmares can only be thrust aside, never defeated. What if one were to survive?

Children of the New Disorder is a chilling fever dream from the mind of *New York Times* bestseller Tim Lebbon. Paired with the refreshing voice of a newcomer, Lebbon's lauded prose has become unexpectedly daring in this spellbinding tale of the horrors around and within us. Coming June 2008.

$35—*Unto Dust* edition: signed, limited to 450 copies.

About the Press

Creeping Hemlock Press was founded in Gretna, Louisiana by the husband-and-wife creative duo R.J. and Julia Sevin (*seh-VAN*). As sometime writers, oftentime readers, they found themselves frustrated with the scarcity of generous-paying, atmospheric and bizarre short story anthologies. They took matters into their own hands in late 2004 when they began to accept submissions for their own anthology. Many months, one baby, two hurricanes, and one soggy home later, *Corpse Blossoms* was born to critical success and a nomination for the Horror Writers Association's Bram Stoker award. As their homeless wanderings carried them to Texas and back, the Sevins also produced an original limited-edition novella by Tom Piccirilli, *Frayed*, to terrific reviews and enthusiastic reader sentiment.

Even before the disaster and reaction surrounding Katrina demonstrated its true meaning, charity was a pillar of Creeping Hemlock Press's philosophy and business model. Each title is paired with a worthy non-profit, which is given 10% of the overall profits from the sale of that title. For more details, visit our website.

Looking to the future, R.J. and Julia are excited about Creeping Hemlock Press's next few offerings, including *The Shallow End of the Pool* and the intriguing *Unto Dust* series of apocalyptic novellas. Visit the Sevins and learn more about the press, if you please, at www.creepinghemlock.com.